KENRIC CAN'T ESCAPE
THE GROWING EVIL....

"Nothing followed ye here, did it?" the gatekeeper asked, peering back down the road.

At the old man's question, Kenric felt as if icy drops of rain were scuttling down his back. The shadows had grown long, their dark shapes eating up the last of the remaining light. "What would have followed me?"

The gatekeeper shrugged. "I don't know. But you have the stink of trouble on ye."

Just then, the sun dipped all the way below the horizon. There was a loud rustle and snarl from the side of the road. Kenric looked at the gatekeeper. "Wha—?"

Three black shapes burst out of the bushes. Hounds. But not like any Kenric had ever seen before. These were enormous. Their thick muscles bunched and stretched as their long, loping strides ate up the distance to the gate. In the fading sunlight, their eyes glowed red. The hounds' mouths hung open as they ran, and Kenric saw rows and rows of teeth heading straight for him.

❧❧

OTHER BOOKS IN THE
LOWTHAR'S BLADE TRILOGY

The Secrets of Grim Wood
The True Blade of Power

LOWTHAR'S BLADE TRILOGY · BOOK 1

THE FORGING OF THE BLADE

LOWTHAR'S BLADE TRILOGY
✦ BOOK 1 ✦

THE FORGING OF THE BLADE

R. L. LaFevers

PUFFIN BOOKS

PUFFIN

Published by the Penguin Group

Penguin Young Readers Group,

345 Hudson Street, New York, New York 10014, U.S.A.

Penguin Group (Canada), 90 Eglinton Avenue East, Suite 700, Toronto,

Ontario, Canada M4P 2Y3 (a division of Pearson Penguin Canada Inc.)

Penguin Books Ltd, 80 Strand, London WC2R 0RL, England

Penguin Ireland, 25 St Stephen's Green, Dublin 2, Ireland

(a division of Penguin Books Ltd)

Penguin Group (Australia), 250 Camberwell Road, Camberwell, Victoria 3124, Australia

(a division of Pearson Australia Group Pty Ltd)

Penguin Books India Pvt Ltd, 11 Community Centre, Panchsheel Park,

New Delhi - 110 017, India

Penguin Group (NZ), Cnr Airborne and Rosedale Roads, Albany, Auckland 1310,

New Zealand (a division of Pearson New Zealand Ltd)

Penguin Books (South Africa) (Pty) Ltd, 24 Sturdee Avenue,

Rosebank, Johannesburg 2196, South Africa

Registered Offices: Penguin Books Ltd, 80 Strand, London WC2R 0RL, England

First published in the United States of America by Dutton Children's Books,

a division of Penguin Young Readers Group, 2004

Published by Puffin Books, a division of Penguin Young Readers Group, 2006

3 5 7 9 10 8 6 4 2

THE LIBRARY OF CONGRESS HAS CATALOGED THE DUTTON EDITION AS FOLLOWS:

LaFevers, R. L. (Robin L.)

The forging of the blade / by R. L. LaFevers.—1st ed.

p. cm.

Summary: Ten-year-old Kenric leaves the village of Penrith to look for his father,

who recently has gone missing, and discovers that the evil Lord Mordig

is plotting to take over the kingdom.

ISBN 0-525-47349-1 (hc)

[1. Fantasy.] I. Title.

PZ7.L1414Fo   2004

[Fic]—dc22   2004001978

Puffin ISBN 0-14-240557-4

Printed in the United States of America

To Mark Lafevers,

whose broad shoulders, strong arms, and warm heart

have forged a bond so powerful that his family

would travel to the ends of the earth and back

should he ever disappear

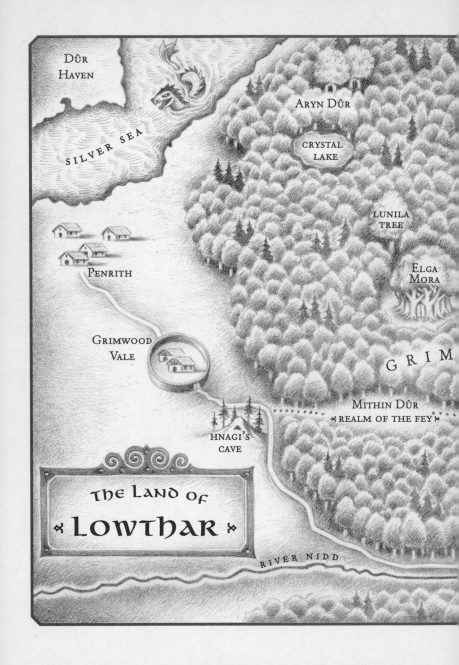

LOWTHAR'S BLADE TRILOGY · BOOK 1

THE FORGING OF THE BLADE

❊ I ❊

IN THE DIM light of the cottage, Kenric stared at the handful of iron nails in front of him. It was all he could scavenge from the smith yard today. Everything else had been sold off for food.

He picked one up off the table and twirled it between his fingers. This was the last thing he and his father had worked on together before his father had disappeared.

If he closed his eyes, he could still remember the feel of his father's hands as they steadied his. He could still hear his father's voice as he gently reminded Kenric to look to the fire. Just then, a group of village lads had run by. He had looked longingly at them and sighed.

His father had gone over and lifted a shovel from the wall. He brought it over to Kenric. "See this simple farm tool? It takes only a few trips to the fire and a little shaping. If it fails or breaks, nothing much will be lost. It is easily replaced."

Then his father pulled an unfinished long sword from his workbench. He had been working on it for months. "The sword blade is a whole different matter. It must be shaped over time and takes many turns at the flame. Its strength and balance are crafted by repetition. Lives and kingdoms will depend on its performance."

Kenric shook his head, confused by his father's words.

His father had laid a rough hand on Kenric's head and ruffled his dark brown hair playfully. "You, my son, are a blade. You must put up with years of shaping and training, where other boys will run free. It is a great gift to be a blacksmith, but a burden as well."

The next day, with no word or warning, Kenric's father was gone.

The back door to the cottage banged shut, breaking into his memories. His mother came in and hung her shawl on the peg by the door. She turned toward Kenric, her hands clasped nervously before her. "Well, I have petitioned the council for my widow's portion," she said.

Kenric's stomach clenched. "Father is not dead."

"Perhaps not, but how else will we get through the

winter?" Her voice was soft, as if she knew her words would cause him pain.

Kenric gripped the nail in front of him. "Some other way," he said. He refused to believe his father was dead. He looked down at the nail he grasped in his fingers. "I've asked the council to let me reopen the forge. If they say yes, then I can carry on doing some of the small jobs Father taught me."

His mother opened her mouth to speak, but was interrupted by a pounding at the door. She frowned. "Who is calling so late?"

Kenric shrugged. He slipped the nail into his pocket and got up from the table.

When he opened the door, a dark, bulky form loomed before him. "Gormley," he said, forcing the words past the knot of worry in his throat.

"That's *Master* Gormley to you, rude pup. Is your mother home?" The large man shoved his way into the cottage. Kenric balled his fists and took a step toward him.

Kenric's mother caught his eye and waved him back. Then she turned to their visitor. "Master Gormley. You do us great honor with your visit."

Gormley smiled, his teeth stained and crooked. "'Tis

no social call. I've come to let you know this cottage has been declared abandoned. You must be gone one month from now."

Kenric's mother gasped, and her hand flew to her mouth. "But it is not abandoned! You can see that with your own eyes! My son and I still live here. We tend the place. Maintain it well. We have honored—"

"There is no man of the house. In the eyes of the law, it is abandoned."

Kenric squared his shoulders and stepped forward. "I am the man of the house. We pay our rents! You have no cause to throw us out."

Gormley threw back his head and laughed. "You are not the man of the house! You're nothing but a scrawny eleven-year-old boy whose father has abandoned him."

"He did not!" The force of Kenric's words scraped at his throat. "Something has happened to him."

"Can ye prove it?" Gormley asked.

Kenric wished he *could* prove it. Then the law would protect his mother and him. There were allowances for widows with children, but none for families who'd been abandoned. Kenric looked down at his feet. "No. But I'm sure of it, just the same."

Gormley smirked. "He left the two of you high and

dry. You pay the rent now, but just barely. What will happen when winter comes? With nothing to sell at market, how will you survive the long cold months?" The man took a step forward until he towered over Kenric. "Then how will I get my rents?"

Kenric spoke up. "The council is going to let me start up the forge. Then I can do some of the smaller jobs. That should be enough, until he returns—"

Gormley put his hands on his hips and scowled. "Wake up, lad. He's not returning! He's gone to seek his fortune elsewhere. Besides, the town council met this afternoon. They will not let you reopen the forge. You are too young. Now"—his cold gaze swept over them—"be gone in one month or I shall drag you out with my bare hands." Then the large man turned and headed for the door.

Kenric's hand went to the nail in his pocket. He wished he could drive it into Gormley's fat belly.

⊰ 2 ⊱

KENRIC LAY AWAKE half the night. Never before had he felt so helpless. Never before had things looked so bleak.

For two months he had hung on to the hope that his father would return any day. He would have a simple explanation for his disappearance.

When Father came back, the whispering would stop. People would no longer point at Kenric and his mother when they went to market. There would be no more ugly rumors or hidden looks. But most important, they would be a family again. Kenric would not have a gaping hole in his life where his father used to be.

Kenric rolled over and punched the lumpy mattress. Why had the town council refused his request to start up his father's forge? Kenric could do the work. He'd been doing it at his father's side for as long as he could remember. Besides, for the last few months his father had been shoveling blacksmithing knowledge at him faster than he could take it in.

Kenric froze. Perhaps his father had known trouble was coming. Perhaps he'd been trying to prepare Kenric for that.

Kenric threw off his covers and sat up. His father had always said that if the answers didn't come to Kenric, then he must go in search of the answers. Very well. Kenric would do exactly that. He would go and find out what had happened to his father.

Faced with a plan of action, Kenric was eager to get started.

When dawn finally peeked through the window, he had just finished packing his knapsack. He shouldered the pack, then made his way to the kitchen as quietly as possible.

He paused at the cottage door, torn. He wanted to say good-bye to his mother and let her know he would be back soon. Hopefully, with Father. And if not, then at least with news of him.

But she would most likely try to talk him out of going. Possibly even forbid it. He couldn't give her that chance. He needed to find his father. He needed to prove to everyone, especially Gormley, that his father hadn't abandoned them.

Kenric stepped out the door and hurried through the streets of Penrith. It was quiet still. The villagers were just now waking up. They would be too busy with breakfast or morning chores to notice him leaving. He wanted his leaving to go as unnoticed as possible.

When Kenric reached the outskirts of town, he let out a sigh of relief.

"Eh lad, where are you headed so early this morning?"

Kenric jerked his head up and saw Farmer Rawley outside his barn, harnessing his oxen. The old farmer waved him over.

Kenric switched directions and headed for the old farmer. "It's Gormley," he said as he drew closer. "He came last night and told Mother and me we have to be out in one month."

Rawley scowled. "Gormley? So soon? But it's only been a few weeks!"

"That's what we tried to tell him. But he wouldn't listen. And the council won't let me work the forge either."

"I'm not surprised. They're afraid, lad."

"Afraid of what?" Kenric scoffed. "That I might be able to take care of my mother and myself?"

The farmer leaned forward and lowered his voice. "These are evil times, boy. They don't want something to happen to you, like it did your da."

Something deep inside Kenric squirmed. "What do you mean?" he asked sharply.

"I mean, there are rumblings from the east. Your father isn't the only blacksmith in Lowthar to go missing. That's what the council is worried about."

Kenric gaped at Rawley's words.

"Now, you'd best be on your way. There's evil afoot. It's not safe to be out on the open road after dark. You'll be lucky to make it to Grimwood Vale before the sun sets."

Kenric shifted his pack but didn't take a step. "What else have you heard?" he asked. "Do they say what happened to the blacksmiths? Where they are now?"

Farmer Rawley shook his head. "I don't know. But you'd best get going." He reached out and gave Kenric a gentle shove. "Stick to the open road and avoid the shadows. You'll be safest that way. And good luck to ye."

PENRITH WAS A small village perched on the western edge of the kingdom. There was only one road leading out of town. Kenric knew the closest village was

Grimwood Vale. Beyond it lay Grim Wood, a large, wild forest that sat in the middle of Lowthar. After that, his geography grew hazy.

His plan was simple. He would follow the road until he bumped into some answers. Surely someone had seen his father pass by two months ago.

Kenric spent the whole day looking over his shoulder. His mind kept running back to Rawley's warnings. He was half-afraid some creature would step out of the bushes and grab him. Or worse yet, he might run into whatever evil was creeping this way. His heart thudded with every rustle in the underbrush. He jerked around every time the wind whispered through the trees.

There were no other travelers on the road. He had expected at least one or two, but there were none. It was hard to believe things were so terrible that no one dared to leave their home.

He finally reached Grimwood Vale at sunset, just as the gates were closing for the night. Having no wish to be stuck out on the open road, Kenric broke into a run. "Wait!" he called out to the gatekeeper.

"What's a puny bit of a lad doing out on the road alone?" the gatekeeper asked when Kenric reached him.

"I'm traveling east. I was hoping to pass the night here

in Grimwood Vale," Kenric huffed as he tried to catch his breath.

"Nothing followed ye here, did it?" the gatekeeper asked, peering back down the road.

At the old man's question, Kenric felt as if icy drops of rain were scuttling down his back. His thoughts flew to Rawley's warnings. He turned to look back down the road. The shadows had grown long, their dark shapes eating up the last of the remaining light. "What would have followed me?"

The gatekeeper shrugged. "I don't know. But you have the stink of trouble on ye."

Just then, the sun dipped all the way below the horizon. There was a loud rustle and snarl from the side of the road. Kenric looked at the gatekeeper. "Wha—?"

Three black shapes burst out of the bushes. Hounds. But not like any Kenric had ever seen before. These were enormous, bigger than Kenric could ever have imagined. Their thick muscles bunched and stretched as their long, loping strides ate up the distance to the gate. In the fading sunlight, their eyes glowed red. The hounds' mouths hung open as they ran, and Kenric saw rows and rows of teeth heading straight for him.

❧ 3 ❧

THE GATEKEEPER JUMPED back and tried to shut the gate. With horror, Kenric realized he meant to leave him outside. Kenric turned and flung himself against the gate, forcing it open enough so that he could scrape through.

The gate slammed shut behind him, catching the hem of his tunic. Behind him, the whole wall shuddered as the hounds hurled themselves against it. They scrabbled and scratched, trying to force their way in.

A vicious tug yanked Kenric back against the gate. There was another strong jerk, then he was free. He whirled around and saw a large piece of his tunic missing. The hounds had come that close! He gulped. Outside the gate, they let loose a bloodcurdling howl that made the back of Kenric's neck prickle.

He whipped around to face the gatekeeper. "You were going to leave me out there!"

The gatekeeper shrugged. "It's my job to keep things out of Grimwood Vale. It was you they were after. Now they'll be howling at the gates all night."

"Wh-what are they?" Kenric asked.

"Mawr hounds, boy."

"Where did they come from?"

"Followed you. Just like I thought."

Kenric frowned. "Followed me? But I didn't see any sign of them on the road."

The old man nodded his head to where the sun had just disappeared. "'Tis the light. They stick to the shadows during the day, then begin their hunting at night."

"How come I've never heard of them before? Why are they hunting me?" Kenric asked.

"Depends," the gatekeeper said as he wiped his nose on his sleeve. "What have ye been up to?"

Kenric opened his mouth to say "Nothing," then stopped. Could Gormley have sent them? No, he thought with a shudder. If Gormley had hounds such as that, surely Kenric would have known about it.

The gatekeeper leaned forward. Kenric wrinkled his nose at the stale, musty breath.

"Those hounds could have gnawed the flesh off your bones, then snatched your soul from your body."

"What do they do with souls?" Kenric asked, holding his breath.

"How should I know? Now get out of here before I decide to open the gate and let them at ye!" With that, the gatekeeper turned and disappeared into the gatehouse.

Kenric looked over his shoulder at the gate. The Mawr hounds continued to yelp and snarl, trying to get in. Ignoring them as best he could, Kenric hoisted his pack and turned toward the town.

He was barely one day out of Penrith and he'd already seen and heard things he could scarcely believe.

As he walked away, the Mawr hounds let loose with another gibbering, ratcheting howl. Up and down the street, doors and shutters slammed shut. It wasn't until the very end of town that he spied a building with a sign shaped like a rooster swinging above the door. The tavern.

As Kenric drew closer, voices spilled out into the night. When he opened the door, all the talking stopped. A room full of faces turned to stare at him, suspicious and unfriendly. Kenric squared his shoulders and made his way to the bar.

The innkeeper behind the counter eyed him with suspicion. "What would you be wanting?" the enormous man asked.

"I'm looking for a place to pass the night," Kenric said.

The innkeeper studied him in an odd way. It looked as if he were counting just how much Kenric would fetch at market. "How much coin have you got?"

Kenric shuffled his feet. "I've no coin. But I can work for my supper and a room. I've strong arms and back." He glanced around the room. "I can carry trays. Serve the drinks. Wash your dishes and pots for you afterward."

The innkeeper narrowed his eyes. "I can do all that myself. I don't need any boy for that." He said the word *boy* as if it were a nasty bit of gristle on his tongue.

Kenric frowned and shifted his pack. He hadn't expected such an unpleasant welcome. "Is there another inn I can try?"

"No. We're not fond of strangers around here."

Kenric wanted to ask why they didn't like strangers, but held his tongue. Living so close to Grim Wood might make them wary. Or maybe it was the evil Farmer Rawley had mentioned.

Trying to hide his disappointment, Kenric turned toward the door. It looked as if he would be sleeping under the stars tonight. At least he would be safely inside the town walls. On the heels of Rawley's warnings, and the Mawr hounds, he was grateful for that much.

Just as Kenric reached the door, the innkeeper called out. "I guess I could let you sleep in the stable. If you've a mind to work for it."

Kenric turned around. "I don't mind hard work."

"Well then, you'd best get to it." The innkeeper tossed an apron at Kenric. He caught it and stowed his pack behind the bar.

"Boy! We need ale here!" a rough voice called out.

Kenric picked up a tray heavy with tankards and moved toward the voice. Four men watched as he set full tankards of ale down in front of them. As he served the men, Kenric cleared his throat. "Do you get many travelers through here?"

"Why do you want to know?" asked a man with a bushy black beard and a scar over one eye.

Surprised at the man's distrust, Kenric shrugged. "I come from Penrith," he said. "Most people don't find much reason to travel to Penrith."

"Eh, that's probably true," the man agreed. "We get a few more visitors than you do." The man turned back to sip his ale.

Kenric wiped his sweaty palm on his apron and took a deep breath. "That's one of the reasons I've come to Grimwood Vale. I'm looking for someone. He would have come through here two months ago. His name is Brogan, from Penrith. He's my father and the blacksmith there."

At the word *blacksmith,* a hush fell over the table.

The man with the beard looked away and wouldn't meet Kenric's eyes. "Nay. Never saw him. Wouldn't tell if I did, either."

"But why?"

"Because 'tis a foul time to be a blacksmith, lad. Now quit with your questions or you'll be out on your ear."

Kenric chewed over the man's words as he made his way back to the bar. This confirmed what Farmer Rawley had told him that morning. Blacksmiths seemed to be disappearing.

As Kenric reached the bar, the man with the beard turned to face the room. "Did any of you hear of Farmer Trott's son?" He spoke to the whole tavern, but his eyes were on Kenric. "He was out hunting in Grim Wood two nights ago and was attacked by wolves."

"How do you know it was wolves?" the innkeeper asked as he placed four full tankards on Kenric's tray.

"Weren't no bones left behind," answered the bearded man.

Another man from a table near the fire spoke up. "Then maybe it was the Fey."

An uneasy silence settled over the room, until the innkeeper spoke again. "What makes you think it was the Fey and not the hounds?" he wanted to know.

All the talk dribbled to a stop. The man near the fire turned pale. "Are the hounds about again?"

The innkeeper speared Kenric with a look. "Yes."

Not meeting the innkeeper's eyes, Kenric lifted his tray. When he heard the door creak open, he turned to look over his shoulder. An old, bearded man came in, leaning heavily on a walking stick. He was dressed in rags of gray and was thinner than a shadow.

A beggar, Kenric realized. Forced to go from door to door, looking for charity. It's what would become of his mother and him if he couldn't find Father.

No one in the tavern turned to look in the old man's direction. He shuffled over to a table in the farthest corner. Kenric made his way over and placed a tankard in front of him. The old man looked up in surprise. "Why, thank you for seeing to an old man's thirst."

"You're welcome," Kenric said.

"Don't believe I've seen you in these parts before."

"You haven't. I'm not from here. I'm from Penrith."

"What's a young lad like you doing so far from home?" the old beggar asked.

Kenric thought of the bearded man's strange words, then pushed them aside. He would learn nothing if he was too afraid to ask questions. "I'm looking for my father. He was the blacksmith from Penrith. He must have come this way two months ago."

Once again, at the word *blacksmith,* those close enough to hear stopped their talking.

"A blacksmith, you say?" There was a spark of interest in the old beggar's eyes that made Kenric think he might know something.

Just then, the inn door crashed open, slamming into the wall. The candles dimmed and the fire sputtered.

Kenric whirled around to see who had come in.

The stranger was tall and thin. He wore a long black cloak that was pulled forward so that Kenric couldn't see his face.

As the man made his way to the bar, a choking fear slowly filled the tavern. The innkeeper grew pale and licked his lips nervously. "Can I help you?"

The tall, cloaked figure didn't answer but instead

turned to the room. "What's all this talk of blacksmiths? Is there a new one in town? And you didn't tell me?"

The innkeeper threw a quick glance at Kenric, then turned back to the stranger. "There's no new blacksmith that I know of."

The hooded stranger turned his back to the bar and let his gaze roam over the room. Finally, it landed on Kenric. Kenric fought down the urge to panic and bolt, and stood his ground.

"What about him?" the hooded figure asked. "Who is he?"

"Who? Him?" the innkeeper asked, his voice wobbly. "Why, he's just passing through. He was looking for a place to pass the night, and I thought I'd let him help out for a bit."

"It's him that was asking about blacksmiths," the man with the black beard and the scar called out.

The hooded figure pushed away from the bar and began walking toward Kenric. Slowly, Kenric's gaze moved up the black cloak to the face staring at him, then he jerked back. The skin was drawn tight against the bone, making the face almost skeletal. The eyes were cold and flat and glittered red. Was it the glow from the fire that made them so? No man could have red eyes.

The stranger stopped in front of Kenric. "What's your interest in blacksmiths?" he asked.

"I—I'm looking for my father," Kenric said.

"He is a blacksmith?"

Kenric nodded.

"And he is missing?"

Again, Kenric nodded.

"Then he is no longer your father. Now forget him and be gone."

Kenric gasped as if the man had struck him. "No! I will not forget him! What do you know of him? Tell me," he demanded. "Do you know who's been taking all the blacksmiths?"

The stranger hissed out a breath and his eyes narrowed until they were two red slits. "Who dares to speak to a Sleäg this way?"

Kenric squared his shoulders and raised his chin. "I do. I am Kenric of Penrith, and I want to know what you've done with my father."

Kenric waited for some of the men in the tavern to stand by him in this. But no one would. They all looked away, unable to meet Kenric's eyes. Their reactions chilled Kenric as much as the cloaked figure in front of him. Who could strike such terror into the hearts of grown men? Their fear made him angry. He turned back to the stranger. "Who are you?" Kenric asked. "What power do you hold over them?"

The cloaked figure sniffed, as if the fear in the room were a fine perfume. "I am a Sleäg and answer only to Lord Mordig. Now men fear me. You would be wise to do so as well." The creature smiled.

Before Kenric could ask any more questions, the Sleäg raised his arm and backhanded him across the face.

Pain exploded in Kenric's cheek. He lost his balance and felt himself falling to the floor. He landed so hard he saw stars dance in front of his eyes. The coppery tang of blood filled his mouth. There was a loud crash as the tray he'd been holding hit the floor. Ale sprayed everywhere.

"Get him out of my sight," the Sleäg said.

Kenric heard the sound of boots clumping on the wooden floor. Suddenly two strong hands reached down and grabbed him in an iron grip. "You fool!" the innkeeper whispered harshly. "Is this how you repay my kindness?"

"I—I . . .," Kenric stammered.

The innkeeper jerked Kenric forward and dragged him to the tavern door. "There'll be Sleäg swarming all over here now, trying to punish us for your boldness," he scolded. "Who knows what horrors they'll heap upon us!"

The innkeeper kicked the door open. Then, lifting Kenric as if he were a sack of potatoes, hurled him out the door into the street.

Kenric hit the ground with a bone-rattling thud that knocked the breath clean out of him. With his face still in the dirt, he heard the tavern door slam shut behind him.

❧ 4 ❧

KENRIC SPIT THE dirt out of his mouth. He eased up slowly. Painful bruises spread through his body, but nothing seemed broken.

He swayed dizzily and tried to get his bearings. The innkeeper had said that more of Mordig's creatures would be coming. Did he mean tonight?

Kenric turned his head around to stare into the darkness for any sign of movement. Nothing. At least not yet.

He took a step forward. Dizziness swirled through him and he stumbled. He looked up and down the village. He needed to find someplace to spend the night. He couldn't stand here like a bump in the road until morning.

As his aching head began to clear, he remembered the innkeeper saying something about a stable. That would do for tonight. Kenric was more afraid of what the dark might hold than of the innkeeper's wrath.

Kenric headed for the back of the inn to look for shelter. He couldn't shake a sense of being watched. Of something out there in the night slowly following him to the barn.

He finally reached the stable and slipped inside the door. The smell of old hay, horses, and cows greeted him. He felt his way along the wall, looking for a pile of hay to sleep on.

He quickly found one and eased his aching body down onto it. If only he'd thought to grab his pack before he'd been thrown out. He would dearly love his bedroll. And the small bit of food he'd packed that morning.

Well, at least there was hay to lie on. As he settled comfortably, his hand went to the nail he still carried in his pocket. The feel of the cold, hard iron gave him strength. He would not give up his search until he found his father.

Just as he began to drift off to sleep, he heard a noise at the doorway. He jerked up. Something *had* followed him.

"Well, now. That was an interesting display," said a voice.

"Who's there?"

The old beggar stepped out of the shadows. "Just I, come to see if I can share your barn with you."

As Kenric's fear ebbed, he found he was glad of the company. "There's room for two."

The old man smiled. "I had hoped there might be."

Kenric studied him in the moonlight. His clothes weren't really in tatters. They were just old and faded. It was as if the man were barely there at all. Kenric noticed again how thin he was, which reminded him of his own hunger. He reached for his pack, then remembered he'd left it in the tavern.

"Looking for this?" the old man asked. Kenric's pack dangled from one bony hand.

"Yes!" Kenric jumped to his feet and reached out for his pack. "Thank you! I'd thought I'd lost it for good."

The old man came farther into the barn, then sat down in the hay. "So, what made you dare to cross the Sleäg?"

Kenric looked up from rifling in his pack. "Sleäg," he repeated, testing the feel of the word on his tongue. It had a foul taste to it. "What *are* they?"

"Agents of evil. They used to be men, once. But the fires of their hatred have scorched away their humanity, and evil takes its place. Now their only joy is in bringing misery to others."

Kenric pulled a packet out of his pack. "Why didn't the men in the tavern stand up to him?" He broke a piece of bread from the loaf and held it out to the beggar.

The old beggar waved away the food. "Because they have families to tend to, crops to bring in, businesses to run. Most can't afford to stand up to the Sleäg because they have too much to lose. Such rebellion won't go unpunished."

Was that what had happened to his father? Kenric wondered. Had he stood up to the Sleäg and now he was being punished? Kenric was finally getting some answers, but they brought more questions.

Kenric took a bite of bread, then spoke around it. "And the hounds?"

"With the right tools, cannot any living thing be turned to evil? Starvation, whippings, taking away all hope will twist and damage even simple hounds. Once they are full of bitterness and hatred, then Mordig makes them his."

Kenric was chilled by the old man's words. "Who is this Mordig everyone is so afraid of? The Sleäg mentioned him as well."

"Well, for one, it is he who has taken all the smiths."

Kenric froze with a bite of bread halfway to his mouth. "Why? What could he want with all those black-smiths?"

A deep sadness filled the old man's eyes. *"Sweat is to make it, blood is to bind it, strike first in love, so evil can't find it."*

"What is that you're singing?"

"A bit of old lore, although some might call it a prophecy."

Kenric leaned forward. "A prophecy of what?"

The old beggar shrugged. "Of what's to come. Or what might have been. Perhaps it would be better if I showed you." Without waiting to see if Kenric would follow, the old man stood and headed outside. Kenric stuffed the last of the bread in his mouth and followed.

The beggar led the way to an old horse trough filled with brackish water. Uneasy, Kenric glanced up at the inn, but all the lights were out. He strained his ears in the darkness, listening for soft, shuffling footsteps or the distant sound of hounds, but all was quiet.

He turned back to the beggar. The old man raised his arm and dragged the trailing ends of his robe across the water's surface. When the ripples stopped, Kenric gasped. There, on the surface of the water where moon-light used to shine, was a forbidding fortress.

He looked up at the old man. "Who are you? *What* are you?"

"Hush now, and listen. This is Tirga Mor, the heart of Lowthar."

Kenric stepped closer.

"Some say Mordig is a warlord who came from the north. Others say the east. No one knows for sure." The old man's face hardened into grim lines. For the first time, Kenric thought to be afraid of him. "Wherever he came from, he is a terrible evil that has fallen over our land.

"He wanted to be the one powerful ruler over the land of Lowthar. To gain this power, he had to kill the right-ful king in order to seize the blade of Lowthar. He needed that sword in order to rule the land."

As the beggar spoke, pictures appeared on the water's surface. Kenric saw a huge, armored figure holding a sword high. He swung it down, striking an older man with a long beard wearing a small gold circlet on his head.

"But after Mordig did this deed, he found that the sword of power had disappeared, along with the murdered king's body. What he didn't know was that the blade had been fully bound to the king's will. Nothing could turn it against him. Not even an evil as great as Mordig's. None of his spies or henchmen had warned him of that." The old man shrugged. "Perhaps none of them knew. It was Mordig's greatest weakness. He did not fully understand the nature of the blade."

"But if the blade was bound to the king's will, how could Mordig have used it against him?" Kenric asked.

"He shouldn't have been able to," the old man said. "It is against everything known about the blade! And yet, he did. I do not understand it." The old man shook his head, puzzled.

"What happened to the king?" Kenric asked softly. "Did he die?"

"The blade smote his body, but this king's spirit was strong. A powerful spirit is not so easily killed. He did not die, but he no longer truly lives, either." The old man started to say something else, then stopped. He turned to face Kenric. "Mordig wanted more than mortal power. He had his agents scour the land, looking for the missing blade. But it was not to be found."

"Why? What was so special about that sword?" Kenric asked.

"Because to be a true king, a ruler must wield the blade of Lowthar. It magnifies the king's will. It gives him full power over the land." The old man sighed, then continued. "Mordig's minions turned to the old lore, looking for answers. They found no hint of what might have happened to the old blade. The last remaining bit of lore anyone has been able to find is what I told you. *Sweat is to make it, blood is to bind it, strike first in love, so evil can't find it.* That is all that remains. Everything else has been forgotten or lost.

"So, with only that bit to guide him, Mordig began his quest to forge a new blade. For without a blade of power, he will never have true dominion over the land."

"The blade of power didn't seem to have done the old king much good," Kenric pointed out.

The old man's face grew thunderous, and he glared at Kenric. "Because he was betrayed! Tricked! And don't forget, he isn't done yet. For all you know, he may be working to take back his throne even as we speak!"

Eager to change the subject, Kenric asked, "What do you know of the blacksmiths?"

"I know that Mordig has called up most of the blacksmiths in his quest to forge this blade. Those who weren't willing were taken by force. He began in the east, near

Tirga Mor, working his way westward. First Craggyness, then Windeyville, Hemsby Heath, then Grimwood Vale, and finally Penrith, the westernmost village in Lowthar."

It was just as Farmer Rawley had said. His father *had* been taken. He hadn't left his family to starve on their own. Kenric's relief quickly disappeared as he realized his father was most likely a prisoner somewhere. "Where do you think Mordig is holding these smiths?"

"At his fortress in Tirga Mor."

The beggar stopped talking and stared deeply into the water trough. As if there were more pictures there that Kenric couldn't see.

Kenric was afraid to ask another question, but he couldn't keep silent. "Why has no one been able to stop Mordig?"

"You saw those men in there. They haven't the courage, or the will. Too much is at stake, and Mordig has grown too powerful."

"But why didn't they stop him earlier?"

"First, he moves in stealth. His agents enter a village, full of sweet talk and promises of wealth and prosperity. All men want to do well by their families, so they hear what they want to hear. It is like eating a rotten apple. Often, you don't realize the fruit is bad until you reach the brown, rotting core. Most do not know what is happening until Mordig already has them in his grasp. They are powerless then. Second, he uses fear and destruction as his tools. His agents travel the countryside, punishing those who refuse to serve him."

Kenric opened his mouth to ask another question, but the old man interrupted him. He spoke gently. "In order to find your father and help him, you will have to travel into the very heart of the darkness itself."

The truth of the old man's words struck Kenric like a sledgehammer. "But how can I . . . ?"

"Just like you confronted the Slcäg, boy. With faith, courage, and a little luck."

"But it would take . . . armies. Weapons. Strength and resources I don't have," Kenric pointed out. Hopelessness filled him. How could he take on someone like Mordig? He couldn't. It was unthinkable. His only hope was to sneak in and be gone before Mordig even realized he'd been there.

"Ah, but cannot a small flame still burn down a house?"

Kenric's mouth dropped open. "Yes," he whispered. Sometimes. If it wasn't smothered or drowned or stomped on first.

"And so you will be a flame of hope in this darkness," the old man said, his eyes fixed on Kenric's face, as if trying to read it.

Kenric felt the weight of the old man's words settle around his shoulders like a leaden cloak. "Who are you?" he whispered.

"A friend of the kingdom. One who has been waiting a long time for someone to take a stand against Mordig. Now come. I will show you the way, and then I must go."

He stepped once more to the water trough and dragged his long, flowing sleeve across the surface. Kenric stared at the sleeve, looking to see what gave it the power to make pictures on water, but he could see nothing unusual. It was just a thin, gray sleeve.

Kenric turned from the sleeve to the water as small pictures began to form there. This image was different from the first one the old man had shown him. This image was still, for one. Nothing moved in it. It took Kenric a moment to realize it was a map.

"This is Lowthar," the old man said. "And here"—he pointed to a small picture of a tower far to the east—"is Tirga Mor, where Mordig lives." The old man brought his finger back to the other side of the trough. "Here is Penrith." His finger drifted eastward and tiny footsteps appeared on the water's surface. "And here, Grimwood Vale. This road will lead you directly to Grim Wood." His finger slowly traced a path from the vale to a thick cluster of green trees. He looked up at Kenric. "You must use the Old Road to get safely through Grim Wood. Once you have left the forest, head directly for Tirga Mor. You will pass roads leading to other towns. Keep to the main road and ignore the others. They lead to ruined villages that will be of no help to you."

Kenric nodded but kept his eyes on the map, trying to commit it to memory.

"Travel safely, my young smith, and may your heart guide the way."

The old man grew quiet. Kenric looked up to ask him a question, but he was gone.

Kenric looked toward the inn, then toward the road. There was no sign of him, which made no sense. He couldn't have gone far.

He retraced his steps to the barn, but it was empty. He leaned his head against the rough wooden wall. His mind was numb from all the unanswered questions. His body throbbed with aches and bruises, while his eyes were heavy with lack of sleep. He stared longingly at the hay. Did he dare try to catch a bit more rest?

He opened his pack to pull out his bedroll. Something small tumbled out from its folds. Kenric bent over and picked it up. He held it to the window, where dawn's first light was just peeking through.

It was a small stone of some kind. He turned it over in his fingers. It was smooth and round and the color of milk. A moonstone?

He'd never seen one before, but he'd heard of them. He'd always thought they were something that had existed long ago and had passed into legend. But here one sat in his hand.

Had the old man—clearly he was much more than a beggar—left it there on purpose? But why? And who was the old man anyway?

Just as Kenric slipped the moonstone into his pocket, he heard a crunch on the gravel. Voices came softly through the night. He crept over to the door and strained to listen.

"I knew the boy was a troublemaker the moment I saw him, Sheriff."

It was the innkeeper! Kenric hurried back over to the hay and picked up his pack. He glanced around, searching for another exit. At the very back of the stable, he spied a small window. It would be a tight squeeze, but he thought he could make it.

He hurried over and tossed his pack through the window. Hoisting himself up onto the frame, he wriggled and squeezed, trying to get through.

Kenric heard the squeak of a rusty hinge as the stable door opened.

With a final push, he shoved his way through the window, scraping his ribs on the sill. He landed on the soft grass, then rolled to his feet. He grabbed his pack and took off running.

❖ 5 ❖

On the road out of Grimwood Vale, Kenric had lots of time to think. He walked among soft rolling hills, colored golden by the rising sun. Fingering the nail still in his pocket, he tried to make sense of all that he had learned.

When he had set out, he had wanted only to find his father. Instead, he had wandered deep into a tangled web of evil. If he wished to see his father again, he would have to march into the heart of it. Knowing his father hadn't abandoned them would make his task easier to bear. Even so, the idea of taking on someone like Mordig seemed impossible.

And yet, what the old man had said was true. A single small flame had the power to bring down an entire cottage.

Kenric's father had been forever telling him that a blacksmith must use hammer and flame to force the iron down the path of his own choosing. Well, this was the path he must choose, and he would use hammer and flame and whatever else was at hand in order to succeed.

He glanced up and saw that his steps had carried him into a small forest. Trees stood on either side of the road, scattering dappled shadows over the trail. His steps slowed as he remembered the hounds from yesterday. He stopped, straining to listen for any signs of them. There was nothing. Perhaps they had given up. Or perhaps they were just waiting. Kenric glanced up at the sky, wondering how much ground he could cover before nightfall. He began walking and picked up his pace. Mindful of the gatekeeper's warning that the hounds stuck to the shadows, Kenric tried his best to avoid them. But it was hard. The shadows were long and spread out over the trail as far as his eyes could see.

BY LATE AFTERNOON, the land had grown harsher. The trees were more gnarled and less green. It was as if they had endured hardships other trees had never known. Boulders and slate thrust up from the ground like dragon's teeth. Their jagged edges forced

Kenric to pick his way carefully across the ground.

He had seen no one all day, not even a cottager. But as the shadows grew longer, he realized he needed to stop and find shelter for the night. He shuddered at the memory of the hounds.

Just as the sun began to dip below the horizon, Kenric spied a large rock formation up ahead that looked like it could be a cave. Adjusting his pack, he switched directions, hoping he might find shelter.

When he reached the formation, he saw that it was indeed a cave. There were no signs of anything living in it, but he wanted to make sure. While a wolf or a bear was less terrifying than any of Mordig's minions, he still didn't wish to sleep with one.

He picked up a small pebble and tossed it into the cave. It clattered loudly in the silence. Nothing came charging out, ready to tear him from limb to limb.

Heartened by this, Kenric stepped up to the mouth of the cave and called out, "Hello?"

Still silence. He wished he'd found this cave when there was enough daylight to fully explore it. But wishes wouldn't give him shelter. Taking a deep breath, he stepped inside.

As he cautiously made his way toward the back, he realized the cavern was deeper than he'd first thought. A flicker of red light on the walls caught his attention. He stepped forward, then froze. A small fire burned in a stone hearth.

It was a small room of some kind. Something's home, just as he'd feared.

Before Kenric could lift his foot to turn around, a voice hissed in his ear.

"Stop. Or I will cut out your heart."

❖ 6 ❖

KENRIC FROZE AS he felt the tip of a blade pressed against his back. A faint burning smell filled his nostrils. He tried to look over his shoulder.

"Be still!" The knife jabbed harder. "What do you wants in my cave, *hu-man*? What have you come to steal from me?"

"N-nothing! I was just looking for shelter for the night."

"Hmm. Likely tale. I wonder if you be tasty?"

Kenric felt a sharp pinch in his upper arm. "Ouch!" Then another pinch on the back of his leg. "Ouch! Stop that!"

"No fat. Stringy meat. I already have plenty of bones. Will just kill you. Leave for wolves. They be thankful."

"No! Don't kill me."

"Why not, *hu-man?* Your people show mine no love."

"Uh, what is your people?"

"Do you not know?" The creature threw back its head and laughed. Kenric choked on its breath, which smelled of rotten meat.

"I am worst night-mare, *hu-man.* I am goblin. I will pinch pieces off you one by one and feed wolves." The creature cackled, then jabbed the point of the knife into Kenric's back again. "Walk. Careful. No tricksie stuff."

Kenric went forward at knifepoint. Goblins! Kenric had thought they were only tales told to frighten children. Not something that truly roamed the earth. His mind searched wildly for some way out of this mess.

The goblin shoved Kenric toward the fire, then scampered over to the hearth. Kenric came face-to-face with his captor for the first time.

The goblin was small, smaller than Kenric. His skin was covered in dirt and soot. It was impossible to tell what color he was underneath all the grime. He had sharply pointed ears and very pointed teeth. Bowlegged, he scuttled sideways when he moved.

"Look," Kenric said when he got over his shock of seeing the goblin. "You don't want to eat me."

"Shsst! Hnagi not want to eat. Wolves do." The little

goblin cackled again. "Now hold still while Hnagi search."

The goblin held the knife in one hand and began patting Kenric with the other. He quickly discovered the lump in Kenric's pocket.

It was the moonstone that the beggar had given him.

"Oo. Treasure," said the goblin. He reached his hand in to pluck it out, then screamed when his fingers touched the stone.

"Ai! Ai! You burn Hnagi! Evil stone in pocket. Evil stone!" The little goblin dropped his knife to clutch his burned hand. He hopped up and down in circles, crying, "Ai! Ai!"

Kenric saw his chance. He leaped for the blade the goblin had dropped. When the goblin saw what Kenric was doing, he also jumped toward the knife.

Kenric got there first.

He scrambled to his feet holding the blade out in front of him. It was oddly made. The handle was carved bone and the blade was carefully sharpened stone.

The goblin took one look at the knife. He squealed, then leaped backward into the fireplace.

"No!" Kenric shouted, trying to stop him. Stunned, he watched as the flames burned all around Hnagi.

"Come out. I promise I won't hurt you. Get out of there now! Before you're burned to a crisp!"

Untouched by the heat of the flames, the goblin poked his head out of the fire. "Nice *hu-man*? You not hurt Hnagi again? Please."

"I don't want to hurt you. I *won't* hurt you," Kenric said. "As long as you don't hurt me. Word of honor."

Hnagi stepped out of the hearth. Kenric stared in disbelief. There was not a burn or scar on him.

"What you want if not hurt Hnagi?"

"How come you're not burned?" Kenric asked. "There's not a mark on you!"

"Goblin secrets," Hnagi said. "Now, what you want?"

"I told you," Kenric said, turning to peer into the fireplace. "I was just looking for a place to spend the night. I was never going to steal anything. Or hurt you. If you let me stay, I'll leave first thing in the morning. I promise." He wasn't happy about spending the night with the goblin, but there wasn't much choice. It was full dark outside, and there was nowhere else to go.

"Hmm." The little goblin narrowed his eyes and pointed to Kenric's pocket. "You not be Fey. Why carry their nasty stone? Are you working for nasty forest Fey?"

"I'm not working for anyone." Kenric stared down at his pocket. "This is a Fey stone?"

Hnagi nodded. "Nasty stone burns goblins."

"I didn't know that. A—friend gave it to me." Kenric asked, "Why doesn't it burn me?"

Hnagi rolled his eyes. "Because you not goblin. Goblin stone not burn you either, but burn nasty Fey."

Kenric leaned forward. "Do you have a goblin stone? Could I see one?"

Hnagi pulled back and studied Kenric. "Why? You will snatch fire-stone. Take it from Hnagi!"

"No! I promise. I just want to see it."

The little goblin rubbed his hands together. A sly look crossed his face. "Turn around, *hu-man*. No peeking."

Kenric turned his back to the goblin and faced the cave wall. He could hear Hnagi scuffling around.

"Here," Hnagi said. There was no mistaking the pride in his voice.

Kenric stepped forward, his jaw dropping. A deep blue stone the size of a large bean sat in the goblin's hand. Fiery red-orange swirls blazed from its depths. Kenric had never seen anything like it. "It's beautiful," he said.

Hnagi swelled at the praise. "It's Hnagi's!"

"I know. May I hold it?"

Hnagi snatched his hand back behind him and scowled. "I just want to see if it burns me, that's all."

Scowling the whole time, the goblin slowly brought his hand out from behind his back. He opened his palm. "Touch. Not hold."

Kenric nodded, then reached out with his finger to touch the fiery rock. It was cold and smooth.

Before Kenric could do more than that, Hnagi closed his fist around the fire-stone and hid it behind his back. "Okay. *Hu-man* saw it. Turn around again."

Kenric did as he was told.

"Where you be going?" the goblin asked.

Kenric hesitated, wondering how much to tell the goblin. "Have you ever heard of someone called Mordig?"

Hnagi slapped his hands over his ears. "Ai! Ai! No Mordig," he wailed. "No Mordig!"

"Stop that!" Kenric said. "Enough! He's not here."

"Mordig everywhere," Hnagi said. There was a haunted look in his eyes. "Mordig mean to goblins."

"Well, he's not very nice to blacksmiths, either," said Kenric. "He took my father, and I'm trying to find him so I can bring him back."

Hnagi began rubbing his hands together. "If *hu-man* is going to fight Mordig, he can stay."

"I'm not going to fight him. I just want to find my father," Kenric explained. At least, he didn't think he was going to fight Mordig. He could never hope to overpower someone like the warlord directly. He would have to use stealth and cunning.

"If Mordig has father, you will fight him. Otherwise, no father," Hnagi said.

Kenric's eyes were gritty from lack of sleep. His head ached fiercely, and his stomach was empty. There was no arguing left in him. "Very well. I guess I'll have to fight him, then. Now may I please stay the night here?"

"Yes. Of course. *Hu-man* Hnagi's honored guest." The goblin scuttled over to the fire and began to unpack the sack he had dropped earlier. He held up two rabbits. "Dinner."

Kenric's mouth began to water at the thought of roasted meat. He sat down on one of the rocky ledges and watched the goblin skin the hares. When Hnagi was done, he turned around and thrust one at Kenric. "Here. For you."

Kenric stared at the raw, skinned rabbit. "Uh. Thanks. But I like my meat cooked."

"You ruin good meat?" Hnagi asked, frowning. "Cook it yourself."

"Fair enough," Kenric said. He quickly located a stick and built a makeshift spit. He put the hare on it, then stuck it in the hearth to roast. He did his best to ignore Hnagi, who grumbled between bites of raw meat.

At least now he knew why the goblin had such horrible breath. It was the old bits of rotten meat that clung to his pointed teeth.

When the meat was cooked, Kenric pulled the stick from the fire. Then he sat down on a rocky ledge and ate greedily.

When he was done, he looked up. Hnagi was watching him.

"What does Mordig do to goblins?" Kenric asked.

Hnagi wrapped his arms around himself. "Mordig big meanie. Kidnaps goblins." He began rocking back and forth. "Makes them dig, dig, dig. Deep in earth. Looking for metal. Metal for blade he wants." Hnagi shuddered. "Very bad to be caught by Mordig."

"Why don't the goblins stop him?" Kenric asked. "You were ferocious enough with me!"

"Not enough goblins. Mordig has armies. Big armies. Lot of evil things fight for Mordig." Clearly upset, the little goblin got down on the ground. He crawled on all fours, circling the hearth three times. Then he collapsed onto the floor with a sigh. Before long, his breathing grew deep and even. Kenric realized he'd gone to sleep.

Exhausted himself, Kenric pulled his bedroll out of his pack. He chose a spot close to the hearth, but as far away from Hnagi as possible.

As he slept, he kept a firm grip on the goblin's dagger.

❉ 7 ❉

KENRIC AWOKE TO find Hnagi sitting on the hearth, watching him.

"*Hu-man* can't catch anyone if sleeping whole day away," the little goblin said.

Kenric leaped to his feet, trying to untangle himself from his blanket. How much time had he lost?

Hnagi threw back his head and laughed. "Is only day-break."

Kenric slumped in relief and resisted the urge to shake the goblin. Fully awake now, he decided it was best to get on the road immediately. If it was light out, there was no use in waiting any longer. He bent over to roll up his blanket and then began stuffing it in the pack.

Hnagi squatted by the hearth. "Does *hu-man* know way through Grim Wood?" he asked.

"More or less. I just follow a path east, right?" Kenric said. He looked down at his belt. The dagger he had taken from Hnagi was gone. The goblin must have taken it back while Kenric was sleeping. Kenric supposed he was lucky it wasn't sticking out of his back.

"Ai. Stupid *hu-man*!" Hnagi stood up. "You will get lost that way. Hnagi show you shortcut. The sooner you kill Mordig, the better."

"I'm not going to kill anyone," Kenric said. "I'm just going to rescue my father."

"Can't have one without the other. You'll see."

Kenric grimaced at the goblin's words. The old man had said much the same thing.

The little goblin scurried over to the hearth. He picked up a handful of soot and ash and put it into a small leather sack.

"What is that?" Kenric asked, frowning.

"Tricksie goblin fire-dust," Hnagi explained. He fastened the pouch to a small leather belt strapped around his waist. The dark, twisted dagger hung at his side as well.

"Why do you need that? Oh! Are you coming with me?"

Hnagi nodded. "*Hu-man* not know what he is doing.

Will show you tricksie goblin shortcut through dark wood."

"Would you quit calling me human? My name is Ken-ric." He'd wanted to argue that he did know what he was doing. But he was painfully aware of just how little he actually knew.

Hnagi paused at the mouth of the cave. He looked long and hard outside at the trees, then scuttled toward the trail. He turned and motioned for Kenric to follow. "Hurry up, Ken-ric."

KENRIC SPENT THE morning watching Hnagi as he darted from shadow to shadow. His path was a wild, crazy zigzag. Finally, Kenric could keep silent no longer. "Isn't it safer to stay out in the sunlight? Why are you sticking to the shadows like that?"

Hnagi looked up into the sky nervously. "Grymclaws," he whispered.

"Grymclaws?" Kenric repeated.

"Shh!" Hnagi hissed.

This was another creature that Kenric had never heard of. He lowered his voice. "What are grymclaws?"

Hnagi held his arms out wide.

"They're big?" Kenric guessed.

The little goblin nodded, then flapped his arms.

"And they fly?"

Hnagi nodded again. Kenric glanced up in the sky before he could stop himself.

Hnagi made a small noise. Kenric looked back in time to see him wave his hand through the air, as if he were snatching something.

"And they snatch things?"

Hnagi nodded wildly, then darted off to the next shadow. Kenric sighed and adjusted his pack. Danger in the shadows; danger out in the open. This was turning out to be more like a nightmare than he could ever have imagined. He only hoped his decision to find his father didn't end up costing him his life.

THEY WALKED THROUGH the morning, not speaking much. Just after noon, they reached an area of the forest where the trees were larger and thicker. Little sunlight penetrated the branches overhead, throwing everything into shadow. Fallen trees covered with moss lay across the faint trail.

Kenric turned to ask Hnagi a question and was startled to find the goblin no longer at his side.

Panic seized Kenric. Had the little goblin fallen behind? Gotten lost? His thoughts flew to the grymclaws Hnagi had been so afraid of. He whirled around, relieved to find Hnagi a few paces back, crouched on the ground, shaking his head.

"You scared me!" Kenric said, his fright making his words harsh. He hadn't realized how responsible he felt for Hnagi until he'd thought him lost.

Hnagi ignored his outburst and pointed at the trees. "We not go that way. No, no. I show you way around."

Kenric looked to the left, then the right. The section of densely packed trees went on as far as his eyes could see. "But won't that take more time?"

Hnagi shrugged. "Yes. But safer. Much safer."

"How much time will it add to the journey?"

Again, Hnagi shrugged. "Two days. Maybe three."

"I don't have that kind of time," Kenric said. Ever since his conversation with the old man, Kenric had felt a need to hurry.

Hnagi scampered over to Kenric. He kept his eyes on the trees as if he expected something terrifying to leap out of them. He reached up and pinched Kenric.

"Ow!" said Kenric, rubbing his arm. "Would you quit that!"

"Not go in there," Hnagi said. "No, no. Bad, nasty

place." He grabbed Kenric's tunic, then stood on tiptoe to get as close to Kenric's ear as he could. "Nasty Fey live here."

So that explained it. This was the part of Grim Wood that the Fey inhabited. And the little goblin was even more frightened of them than the men of Grimwood Vale were.

Kenric's hand moved to his pocket and began fiddling with his nail. Despite everyone's fears, he was willing to risk the Fey. They couldn't be as terrifying as the hounds or Sleäg. Kenric couldn't afford the extra days; he was certain of that. The old man's warnings rang in his head. *Hurry, hurry, hurry.*

He would risk the Fey. He had managed to avoid the Mawr hounds and grymclaws so far. Perhaps he could avoid the Fey as well. He just needed to convince Hnagi that going through Grim Wood was safe. Or as safe as any road was these days.

He turned back to Hnagi. "Won't the trees hide us from the grymclaws you talked about? Wouldn't that be a good thing?"

Reluctantly, Hnagi nodded. "Yes. But nasty Fey no better than grymclaws. Will do terrible, terrible things to Hnagi."

"What about me?" Kenric asked. "Do they hate humans as much as they hate goblins?"

The little goblin shrugged. Kenric found himself growing angry. "Well, they don't own the forest, do they? It's not theirs to keep people out of!" He turned and strode toward the trees. Hnagi, still holding on to his tunic, trailed behind him.

The little goblin tugged frantically. "Look! Look!" he cried, pointing to a fallen tree that lay on the edge of the thicket.

Kenric reached down and removed Hnagi's hand from his shirt, then edged forward to examine the tree. Just behind it was a small clearing with a dozen crudely made crosses. Kenric felt all the blood drain out of his face as he realized they were graves.

Hnagi's eyes were huge in his face and he was trembling so badly his ears shook. "Warnings."

A cold sliver of fear wormed its way down Kenric's spine. He forced himself to shrug it off. "Look. I've got to get to my father as soon as possible. I'm going to cut through the woods. Do you want to come with me or not?"

Eyes still huge, Hnagi shook his head and backed up a few steps. "No," he whispered. "Hnagi not go in there.

Will meet on other side." The goblin turned his back to Kenric and took a few steps away.

"But I can't take the time to wait for you," Kenric called out after him.

"You lucky to make it to other side," Hnagi said over his shoulder, then scampered off.

Hnagi's warning nearly caused Kenric to change his mind. Fear sat in his belly like a cold, hard lump. He took a deep breath and pushed the goblin's words aside.

IT WAS QUIET in this denser part of the forest. There were no twittering birds, no rustling in the underbrush. The air was heavy and still, as if the forest were waiting. And watching. It was an eerie, dreadful place. Kenric had to keep a firm hold on his fear lest it run away with him.

The fine hairs on the back of Kenric's neck rose up and he shivered. He spun around. But there was nothing behind him. At least nothing he could see. Hnagi's warning ran through his mind, but he shoved it aside and forced himself to keep walking.

It was slow going as Kenric worked his way around the trees. The Old Road was nothing but a wildly overgrown path. The branches overhead blocked out most of the light, so it was even harder to see. Kenric hoped he was sticking to an eastward course, but he couldn't be sure.

As the day wore on, the shadows of the trees began to grow longer. What little sunlight filtered down through their leaves disappeared. Dusk was coming. Unbidden, thoughts of hounds and grymclaws, creatures with flame-red eyes, sprang to his mind. Would they dare to enter Grim Wood? Or were they, too, afraid of the Fey? Kenric shivered, not sure he wanted to know the answers to those questions.

He needed to find shelter for the night. Soon.

He hadn't seen any caves in this part of the forest, only the huge, gnarled trees. He looked around and sighed. There was little choice. He looked up into a nearby tree and studied the sturdy branches. It would have to do.

He hauled himself up into the tree and found a thick, solid branch. If he sat with his back to the trunk, he would be fairly secure.

He settled himself on the branch, then put his pack in front of him. He pulled out the blanket and settled it around his shoulders. Then he tied the straps of his pack firmly to the branch. This gave him another idea.

With a grunt, he leaned forward and took off his belt.

It wasn't long enough to go all the way around the trunk. Instead, he wrapped it around his leg, securing himself to the tree branch. If he fell during the night, at least he wouldn't tumble all the way to the ground.

Satisfied, he settled himself against the trunk. He liked the feel of rough, solid wood at his back. He peered down at the ground below. Even a tall hound standing on his hind legs couldn't reach him.

Darkness fell quickly, as if some giant had snuffed out a candle. Kenric saw a few stars winking through the treetops, but they barely pierced the darkness. He hoped the moon would rise soon.

He heard a faint crunch on the ground below. His heart thudded once, then began hammering in his chest. He peered down to the forest floor. "Hnagi?" he called out in a whisper.

There was no answer. What had made that noise? Try as he might, he could see nothing in all that blackness.

He listened, waiting for another sound that would hint at the creature's size or location. But all was silent.

Kenric was surprised at how much he missed the little goblin. He hadn't realized what a comfort it was to have someone else making this journey with him. He wondered where Hnagi would sleep tonight. Could he climb trees? Would he? Or would he burrow in some badger hole somewhere and wait until morning?

Finally, with nerves strung tight, Kenric fell into an uneasy sleep.

KENRIC CAME AWAKE, instantly alert. Something was near. Even with his eyes closed, he could sense a body nearby. He smelled something as well. It was light and green, like a fresh spring breeze.

Careful not to move anything else, he opened his eyes.

A pale arm, glowing in the moonlight, was reaching down from the branch above him. It was moving toward his chest pocket.

Without stopping to think, he reached out and snagged the glowing arm.

Kenric stared at the pale light spilling out between his fingers. He looked up into the branch above him. Two leaf-shaped eyes that were the color of new spring grass stared back at him.

If he wasn't mistaken, he had just captured a Fey. Whatever that was.

❧ 8 ❧

"LET GO OF my arm." The voice danced along Kenric's ears. He found himself wanting to do exactly as the creature said. Instead, he tightened his grip.

"You were going to steal something of mine." He glanced down at his chest pocket. He gasped when he saw the moonstone glowing through the fabric.

"It was not to steal," the Fey said. "I just wanted to see what pretty bauble you carried."

"Very well," Kenric agreed. "But I'll get it. If you don't mind."

The Fey nodded, and Kenric let go of its arm. He was surprised to see his own palm still glowing, as if it were coated in elf dust. There was a rustling in the branches above him, then the Fey dropped down to the lower branch and sat across from him.

She was slightly built. Twigs and leaves stuck out of her reddish brown hair, as if she'd rolled in leaf mold. Her face was foxlike, thin and sharp, and a little wild looking, with sharply pointed ears. Her tunic was woven out of tree bark, leaves, and feathers.

Kenric reached into his pocket and took out the moonstone. It glowed brilliantly in the moonlight.

There was a faint flutter in the night around him. As he looked up, glowing heads peeked out from the branches of the nearby trees. Nearly a dozen of them. They, too, were covered in twigs and leaves so that it was hard to tell where the tree ended and the Fey began.

"He has a luna-lith, Linwe," a voice called out. "It guarantees safe passage."

Safe passage. Was that why the old man had given it to him? Had he known he would need it to get through Grim Wood? It seemed likely.

The Fey girl frowned at Kenric. "How do you come to have a luna-lith? You are not Fey. By what right do you carry it?"

"It was given to me. As a gift."

Linwe turned and spoke to the others in a strange musical tongue. After a bit, one of the other Fey called out, "Who gave it to you?"

"An old man," Kenric told them. "I met him on the road. He gave it to me in exchange for some food I shared with him."

There was more whispering. The older Fey spoke again. "There are a few humans who carry the Fey stone. It is not impossible that you came upon it in this manner."

A look of outrage passed over Linwe's face. She and the older Fey began to argue in their strange language. After a few moments, she turned back to Kenric, scowling. "Old Cerinor would love to get his hands on you. *He* could find out how you came by the luna-lith, and who you stole it from. And a few other things besides."

"I didn't steal it! It was given to me. Besides, he said it guaranteed safe passage!"

"Only if we feel like playing by the old rules," Linwe said. She leaned forward on the branch and poked her face up close to Kenric's. "And very few play by the old rules anymore. Haven't you heard?"

"Enough, Linwe! Your courage is admirable, feyling, but he has earned his safe passage."

"Faroth says because of the luna-lith we must let you go. They always spoil my fun." She sighed so sadly that Kenric almost laughed.

Linwe frowned. "What brings you to Mithin Dûr un-invited?"

"Mithin Dûr?"

Linwe swept her hand in an arc, indicating the forest around them. "Our woods."

"You mean Grim Wood?"

Linwe wrinkled her nose. "That is what you humans call it."

"I didn't know that I needed an invitation."

The Fey's eyes widened. "Do your people wander into one another's homes without permission?"

"No. But I was just passing through."

"Where are you traveling that you must pass through Mithin Dûr?"

Kenric glanced around at the Fey faces poking out from behind the trees. "I am searching for my father," he explained.

"He is missing?" Linwe asked.

Kenric nodded. "He has been taken by Mordig," he said. "He is a blacksmith."

At the name Mordig, a small rustle rose up from the other Fey. The forest dimmed as they all pulled back behind the trees.

Linwe glanced over at the hiding Fey. "Cowards," she

muttered. She turned back to Kenric and handed him the moonstone. "You are brave if you seek to challenge Mordig. It is good that you have the luna-lith. You will need it more than most."

Fumbling a bit, Kenric put the moonstone back in his pocket.

Linwe said, "How do you plan to avenge your father?"

Kenric didn't have a plan. Not yet. But he wasn't about to admit this to Linwe. "I don't plan to avenge him. I only want to rescue him and bring him home."

"If he is still alive," Linwe added.

Kenric fought back a sense of impending doom. "Would Mordig have killed him?" The old man had said nothing of that.

The Fey girl shrugged. "It depends on whether or not he's had his chance at the blade."

Another Fey called out from behind his tree in their musical tongue. Linwe looked over her shoulder, then turned back to Kenric. "Something has followed you here. It is not safe. Hurry out of here like a little mouse while we clean up the mess you've brought us."

This Fey girl was annoying, Kenric thought. He opened his mouth to tell her so but was interrupted by a bloodcurdling yowl. There was more scuffling and rustling, then two Fey emerged from a thicket. They were carrying something between them. Kenric peered down at the forest floor to see what they'd captured.

The creature was small and dark and wailing. "Ai! Ai! No hurt Hnagi! Please, nasty Fey! Don't hurt Hnagi!"

Before Kenric could say anything, one of the two Fey holding him gave him a shake. "You'll get what you deserve!"

"No! Stop!" Kenric called out. "He's with me."

"Traitor!" Linwe accused. Before Kenric could blink, she whipped a long, pointed dagger out of her belt and held it to his neck. He jerked his head back against the tree trunk as the tip of the dagger pricked his skin. He felt a thin trickle of blood run down his throat.

"No! I'm not a traitor," Kenric rushed to explain. "Hnagi is my guide. He's showing me the way to Mordig. I could never have found the way on my own."

"Now that is something I believe," Linwe said. "You humans have rocks for brains."

Kenric tried to look down at Hnagi, but Linwe's blade was in the way. "I thought you were going to go around," he said to the little goblin.

"Got worried about Ken-ric," Hnagi said. "Afraid you'd get lost. Get attacked by nasty Fey."

Kenric wished Hnagi would quit calling them nasty, as if it were part of their name. It didn't seem wise to provoke them just now.

One of the elder Fey called out from the next tree over. "Cerinor has been sent for. We will hear what he has to say before passing judgment."

Kenric tried to take a deep breath, but stopped when he felt the knife press harder against his throat. He could hear Hnagi below, whimpering quietly to himself.

He was touched that Hnagi's concern for him had driven him into the much-dreaded Grim Wood. However, he couldn't help thinking things would have gone much better if the goblin had kept to his original plan.

9

KENRIC DISCOVERED THAT time passed slowly with a blade pressed to one's throat. After a very long while, he spotted a glow moving between the trees. Soon a tall figure emerged. Well, it was tall for a Fey, who seemed to be smaller than humans but taller than goblins. This Fey seemed old. Perhaps it was the long white beard. Or maybe it was the deep lines etched in his face. Whatever the reason, Kenric felt as if he were looking at the oldest living thing he had ever seen.

All the Fey bowed their heads when he appeared. Even Linwe relaxed her hold on the knife and bowed her head.

The man below waved his staff in a circle. One by one the Fey climbed down from the trees and sat around him. Linwe waved her dagger at Kenric. "Come on. Down with you. And don't try anything clever."

Kenric unstrapped his belt from around his leg and began climbing out of the tree. Linwe kept her dagger pointed at him, which made the climb tricky. There was a good chance he'd end up skewered on Linwe's knife, if he didn't fall to his death first.

When he finally reached the forest floor, a wave of relief surged through him. He felt much safer and in control with his feet firmly on the ground.

Linwe landed beside him. She motioned for him to take a place in front of Cerinor, so he did. He beckoned for Hnagi to join him, but Linwe stopped him. "We'll have no goblin fouling our circle. He waits outside."

"What puzzle has found its way into our midst?" Cerinor asked. His voice was heavy with age, but held the promise of wisdom.

Linwe stepped forward. "I found an intruder while patrolling tonight. He has a luna-lith, but I think it was stolen. Then we found he had a goblin with him. He'd brought a *goblin*"—she spat out the word—"into Mithin Dûr! He should be made to pay for this insult!"

Cerinor held up his hand and she stopped talking. She raised her chin and glared at Kenric, as if she could punish him by her gaze alone.

Who did she think she was, anyway? Kenric wondered. She acted like a queen, even though he didn't think she was more than a year or two older than he was.

Cerinor turned his eyes to Kenric. They were a deep, deep green, like leaves in the height of summer. Kenric tried not to flinch as the older Fey studied him. At last, Cerinor spoke. "So, by what twist of fate do you come to possess a luna-lith?"

Kenric repeated the story he had told Linwe and the others.

Cerinor's scrutiny grew more pronounced. "Can you describe this man to me?"

Kenric found the whole story bubbling up from inside him, as if this Fey had the power to call up truth.

When Kenric had finished, Cerinor tapped his fingers on the top of his staff. "It is possible he has come by the luna-lith in this manner. Once, long ago, the Fey shared their moonstones with those who'd earned our trust. We must guarantee him safe passage as is custom."

"B-but he brought a goblin!" Linwe stuttered in outrage. "Doesn't he have to pay for that?"

Cerinor turned his weighty gaze to Hnagi, who shrank down between the two guards holding him. "It has been a long time since a goblin has walked in Mithin Dûr."

"Goblins have never walked in Mithin Dûr!" Linwe argued.

Cerinor turned to her and lifted one shaggy eyebrow. Her mouth snapped shut.

"Once," Cerinor continued, "many generations ago, goblins walked freely in Mithin Dûr."

"Never!" a voice called out.

"Oh yes. There are few left who remember, but goblins and Fey were friends once, long ago."

Voices rose up, muttering among themselves as they digested this news.

"Besides," Cerinor continued, "he is a very *small* goblin. What harm can he do?"

"But we are at war with the goblins," Faroth called out from where he sat in the circle.

Cerinor shook his head. "No. We are not at war with the goblins. We have fallen out of peace with them. That is an entirely different thing."

No one seemed to know what to say to that.

Cerinor motioned to Hnagi. "What is your name, goblin?"

"H-Hnagi, O most honored nasty Fey."

Kenric groaned.

"Come here, Hnagi."

The two guards released their hold on the goblin. Unsteady, he took a step forward. Kenric could see his knees were knocking together.

"Do you wish us harm?" Cerinor asked, his eyes boring into the goblin.

Hnagi shook his head frantically. "No, no. No harm to nasty Fey. Hnagi promise. Just get Ken-ric safely out of forest."

Cerinor studied Hnagi, as if reading the truth from his body. The elder Fey's gaze turned to study the small pouch Hnagi carried at his waist. Kenric thought he saw an orange glow around the pouch. He blinked, and it disappeared.

"Do you carry an igni-lith with you into Mithin Dûr?" Cerinor murmured, almost to himself.

Hnagi clutched his pouch fiercely. He shook his head so hard his pointed little ears flapped back and forth. "No, no. Only goblin dust. No igni-lith."

Cerinor pursed his lips. "We shall see. Very well. Since you travel with someone carrying a luna-lith, we will grant you safe passage through our forest."

Next to Kenric, Linwe huffed out a breath and stomped her foot in frustration. Cerinor whirled about and faced her. "And you, feyling, have much to answer for. You have wrongfully accused this human of treachery. You must make up for that. How do you plan to repay him for your mistaken accusations?"

Linwe's mouth hung open for a brief second before she began spluttering. "P-pay him? For trying to protect Mithin Dûr?"

"No. For making a hasty decision without weighing all the facts. Hurry up and decide. These travelers must be on their way."

Linwe glanced frantically around the grove, looking for help or support from the Fey gathered there. There were many sympathetic faces, but no one spoke up.

Kenric almost felt sorry for her. Almost.

"Hurry," Cerinor urged.

She glanced down at herself. Her eyes went to her dagger, and she gripped it more firmly. She reached into one of her pockets, then fished around in the other. "I— I have nothing to give," she confessed to Cerinor.

The elder Fey grew even more serious. "I think you do," he said. He looked pointedly at the small pouch that hung from Linwe's neck.

She reached up and grabbed the pouch. "No!" she protested. "It was not that great an offense."

Cerinor's voice boomed through the clearing. "Not that

great an offense! What if you had held him here? Killed him, perhaps? Broken the luna-lith promise of safe passage? What then, feyling? Besides"—his voice softened—"I warned you it would only be yours for a little while."

A worried, uncertain look passed over Linwe's face. She started to shake her head.

"Ripples in a pond, Linwe," Cerinor said. "You never know where they will cast up the most innocent of intentions."

Linwe glanced from Cerinor to Kenric. Slowly, she lifted the small pouch from her neck. She held it in her hand a moment, then opened it. She reached in and pulled out something. It was too far away for Kenric to see what it was.

Cerinor motioned her forward. She took three steps until she was directly in front of Kenric. "Here," she said grudgingly. "Cerinor says I must give this to you."

"Linwe." Cerinor's voice growled in warning.

"I'm sorry I wronged you by calling you traitor and doubting your word. Especially since you carried the luna-lith." She glanced over at Cerinor, who nodded his approval.

She held out a small, flat, dark green stone toward Kenric.

This? This is what she was so loath to give up? Kenric reached for the stone. When his fingers touched it, bright red drops blazed up on the green surface. Both he and Linwe gasped. Kenric turned to Cerinor with a question in his eyes.

"It is a blûd-lith, lad, a bloodstone. It belongs to humans, just as the luna-lith belongs to the Fey. When it is held by one of human blood, the stone responds, just as you have seen. You should have it by rights, not an impudent feyling girl."

Kenric stared at the red drops that looked like bright blood spilled on the stone. "If it is human, how do you come by it?"

"I found it," Linwe said. "Several years ago. Near the eastern edge of the forest. Someone must have dropped it." She shrugged.

"But it is a bloodstone and so belongs in the hands of men," Cerinor said. "Perhaps it will be of some use to you on your journey. We Fey have no love for Mordig and hope you succeed."

"If you hate Mordig, why don't you fight him?" Kenric asked before he could stop himself. "Your powers are great."

Cerinor turned his gaze to Kenric. "Once, many years

ago, we would have fought him. But no more. We keep to ourselves now. We tend to our own world here in Mithin Dûr. It is safer that way."

"What happens when Mordig finds his way here?" Kenric blurted out.

Cerinor raised an eyebrow at Kenric. "He can't. Our wards of protection are too strong." He glanced up at the sky. "It is almost daybreak. You should be safe enough. Go now, and may elfspeed bless your journey."

Kenric looked around at the pale, shining faces. "Thank you," he whispered. Then, one by one, they disappeared, like candles being put out for the night.

❈ 10 ❈

KENRIC AND HNAGI were silent as they walked among the towering ancient trees. It felt to Kenric as if the trees themselves were alive. There was a watchfulness to their presence. A thoughtfulness to the rustling of their branches. It wasn't until noon that the travelers cleared the thickest part of the woods. By midafternoon, the trees grew more scattered, and Kenric was sure they must be close to the eastern edge of the forest. Even so, Hnagi continued to cling to Kenric like a cocklebur. When Kenric had tripped over the little goblin for the second time, he thought about scolding him. But he couldn't. Not when he'd bravely risked so much to assure Kenric's safety. Kenric cleared his throat. "I never did thank you for coming into Mithin Dûr after me."

Hnagi trembled and rolled his eyes up at Kenric.

"Hnagi almost get killed by nasty Fey. But most honorable nasty Fey save Hnagi. Save Ken-ric from nasty Fey girl."

"Maybe you should stop calling them nasty, do you think?"

Hnagi stopped walking. "You mean, they don't like being nasty?"

"Well, I don't think they like it, no. I'm sure they don't think of themselves that way."

"Ai! Ai! Why you not cut out Hnagi's tongue?"

Kenric laughed. He couldn't help it. "I wanted to, trust me. But we did all right."

Hnagi shook his head and moaned. "Hnagi should have stayed in nice safe cave. That's where Hnagi belongs."

Kenric started to reply to this but was cut short when a shrill, piercing cry rang out. He stopped walking so suddenly that Hnagi smacked right into him. The cry came again.

Hnagi's eyes grew as big and round as saucers. "Grymclaws!" he whispered.

Kenric looked to the side of the road, searching for cover. Another cry rang out, much closer this time.

"No!" Hnagi squealed. "Mordig's servants have found us!"

A loud rushing sound of air through huge wings filled Kenric's ears. He dove at the little goblin, knocking him off his feet. Still holding on to him, he rolled his way to a thick bush at the side of the road. A flurry of rushing air, feathers, and talons reached them. Kenric ducked, covering his face with his arm.

A bloodcurdling squeal rang out. Kenric jerked open his eyes just in time to see Hnagi lifted high into the air. The winged creature that had seized him was terrifying. Black vulture's wings and body were topped with the head of a hideous hag. Hnagi kicked his feet and tried to wriggle out of its grip, but it held fast.

"Help me, *Ken-ric!* Help me!" the little goblin cried. He continued to struggle, but it did no good. The grymclaw rose high into the sky, carrying Hnagi with it.

"Hnagi! No!" Kenric called out. He sat, stunned. "No," he whispered. It couldn't be. One moment Hnagi had been safe under the bush; the next, snatched away. And it was all Kenric's fault. Guilt, black and bitter, rose up in his throat until it nearly choked him.

The goblin would never have ventured from his cave if not for Kenric. He'd risked Mithin Dûr and the Fey, all of his worst nightmares, so he could help Kenric. He was one of the few who'd offered any help at all. And

Kenric had repaid him by letting him get captured.

The guilt settled in Kenric's gut like lead as the huge bird lifted the goblin high into the sky. Hnagi's cries grew faint.

Suddenly something fell, and for one heart-stopping moment, Kenric thought it was Hnagi. He scrambled out from under the bush and ran to the spot where the object had landed.

Hnagi's belt. Had it come off by accident? Or had Hnagi dropped it on purpose, knowing that Kenric could use the dagger?

When he lifted the belt, he saw the pouch dangling next to the dagger. He remembered Hnagi putting soot and ashes in there. Tricksie goblin fire-dust, he'd called it. Maybe that would be of some use, too.

Then Kenric remembered the strange glow the pouch had given off last night. He quickly untied it and looked inside. Ashes and soot, just as he thought. Gingerly, he stuck in a finger and poked around in the dust until he felt something hard. Slowly, he pulled it out.

It was Hnagi's fire-stone.

Kenric stared back up at the sky, certain now that the goblin had dropped his belt on purpose.

❧ II ❧

KENRIC WALKED FOR two more days, stopping long enough only to rest or eat. At the end of the second day, he reached Tirga Mor just as darkness was falling. His feet were raw with blisters, his muscles screaming with fatigue. He needed to locate shelter for the night.

He glanced up at the fortress towering above him. Its walls of harsh gray stone were cloaked in shadow, as if even the sun were afraid to shine on them. Jagged turrets loomed against the sky like sharp, pointed teeth. The clouds above glowed dull red, lit by some fire burning deep within the belly of the fortress.

Kenric shuddered and turned back to the village that huddled at the base of the fortress. It was deserted. The fields lay bare, with no crops or oxen in sight. He started walking. Someone peered from behind half-closed shutters. Kenric thought about calling out a greeting, but the stillness of the town stopped him. No one came forward in welcome. No one challenged him or demanded he state his business. Living so close within Mordig's shadow had made them fearful.

Kenric left the main road and searched among the out-buildings for a place to sleep. He found a deserted barn at the end of the village. It would have to do.

He soon discovered there wasn't even hay to sleep on. Sighing, he pulled his blanket from his pack and lay down on the cold, hard dirt. As he curled up with his back to the wall, his hand slipped into his pocket. He felt the nail in his fingers. Tomorrow, he thought. He would find his father tomorrow.

KENRIC WAS RELIEVED when the first hint of dawn lightened the sky. Since there was no breakfast to be had, it didn't take him long to get started. Keeping mostly to the shadows of the houses and buildings, he made his way to the fortress. The harsh granite walls were impossible to climb. He quickly discovered that all the doors and gates were heavily guarded. If he wished to get in without being seen, he'd have to look to the drains.

With this in mind, Kenric trudged around toward the

back. A screech sounded in the air above him. Recognizing it immediately, he dived for cover under a nearby bush. With a loud *whoosh,* a grymclaw lunged by. Kenric cringed, not breathing again until he saw her rise up in the air with nothing but branches in her talons.

Kenric sat under the bush and watched as the grymclaw flapped her way back to the fortress.

More cautious now, Kenric made his way to the south end of the fortress. He smelled the drains long before he could see them. He stopped to pull his tunic up over his mouth and nose, then scrambled down the small slope that led toward the drainage ditch. The drains sat low to the ground, a putrid gurgle of filthy water trickling out. When he drew closer, he saw that they were covered with iron bars. His hopes crashed as he realized they were too close together for him to slip through.

Kenric growled in frustration. He had not come this far to give up. He pulled Hnagi's knife from its sheath and went to kneel in front of the drain. Ignoring the stinking, stagnant water, he put the knife to the bar and began sawing.

Soon sweat dripped down his brow, but he ignored it and kept sawing. Finally, when it blurred his vision, he stopped to wipe his face. He leaned closer to see how deeply the knife was cutting. Frustration thick enough to choke him clogged his throat when he saw how little effect the knife had had against the iron.

Another shadow flitted overhead, and Kenric scrambled off to the side to duck behind a nearby boulder. Wasn't it bad enough he'd have to saw for three days to make his way into the fortress? Did he really need to be dogged by grymclaws all morning? Wretched creatures.

Wait! The grymclaws! That was it. They would be his way in.

Shoving the knife back into its sheath, he stepped from behind the boulder into the open. He began waving his arms and shouting, "Hey, you ugly beast! Down here! Here I am! Come and get—"

Faster than he would have imagined possible, the grymclaw turned in the air and swooped toward him. Her gray hair streamed behind her in stringy banners. She rushed in on the wind until she was close enough that Kenric could look straight into her pale, bulging eyes. The foul stench of carrion surrounded him, then there was a blinding rush of wings and feathers. Burning pain burst through him as the grymclaw's talons went clear through his pack and into his shoulders. He screamed. Changing his mind, he tried to twist out of her grasp, but it was too late.

With her talons firmly anchored, she flapped her great black wings and slowly rose back into the sky. Kenric's stomach rolled upside down and threatened to spill out of him. Then he made the mistake of looking down.

The ground! So far away! His stomach looped dizzily again and he hoped he wouldn't be sick.

Flapping her great wings, the grymclaw circled back around until she was close to the fortress wall. The dark stone loomed so close, Kenric was afraid he would smash into it. He screwed his eyes shut. At the last moment, the grymclaw screeched, then veered sharply upward and headed for a turret at the far side of the fortress.

Kenric's shoulders ached and burned. Blood trickled down his arms. He had to think of something, quickly, before they landed.

He groped at his waist, trying to find Hnagi's knife. At last his hand wrapped around the handle. Now he just had to hope he wasn't smashed flat when the grymclaw landed.

As they drew closer to the turret, Kenric saw that two sides of the tower were left open to the air. The grymclaw raced for one of these, then dipped inside. Kenric saw large wooden perches anchored to the floor. Bones lay everywhere in jumbled heaps.

The grymclaw let go. The stone floor rushed up to meet him. He just had time to get his arms up to protect his head before he hit. The impact knocked the breath out of him and he lay for a moment, gasping like a hooked trout.

The grymclaw finished her landing, then turned toward Kenric. He pushed himself to his feet, shrugging out of his pack. His dagger was firmly in hand when she came for him, razor-sharp beak snapping.

He jabbed back. The grymclaw screeched and flapped her wings. Kenric jabbed again, and this time she stepped back, slightly unbalanced.

Pressing his advantage, Kenric took quick, vicious stabs at her chest and belly. He tried to avoid her eyes, her face. It reminded him too much of an old woman who'd lived a hard life. He wasn't sure he could fight the creature if he had to look into her eyes.

The grymclaw screeched again and rose up from the floor onto one of the perches. For the first time, Kenric noticed there were half a dozen other grymclaws. They all sat on their perches, watching, waiting.

The attacking grymclaw launched herself from her perch toward Kenric, talons out.

Just before she struck, Kenric thrust the pack up between them like a shield. Her claws sank deeply into the pack, and Kenric whipped the straps around her ankles, trying to tangle her.

It worked. She fluttered to the ground and stumbled over the pack. Before he could think too much, Kenric raced over and stabbed the knife deep between her shoulder blades.

The grymclaw squealed. The tower rang with the sound of it. Dark blood oozed up from her back.

Before Kenric could congratulate himself on his success, the grymclaw wheeled around and slashed at him with her beak. Kenric leaped back, and found his back against the stone wall.

The grymclaw screeched out her rage and limped toward him, dragging the pack with her. He needed something to fight with. He looked around. Nothing but bones. Without letting himself wonder what kind of bones they were, he reached down and grabbed hold of one. It must have belonged to a leg, for it was narrow and long. He tested the weight of it in his hands, then pulled it back to strike.

The grymclaw was in front of him now. Furious, her eyes blazed. She cocked her head back for one final jab.

Kenric swung the bone toward her head. It connected with a sickening thud. The screech came to an abrupt stop. Fury left the grymclaw's eyes as she crumpled to the ground.

Kenric stood, breathing heavily. There was a rustle around him, and he looked up to see that the other grymclaws had grown restless. They shifted on their perches, eyes darting from Kenric to their fallen sister.

He'd been so intent on the attacking grymclaw, he'd forgotten about the others. The closest one fluttered down from her perch and stepped forward. Another followed, then another. Soon, all six grymclaws were slowly heading toward him.

He could never take them all. He glanced around, frantically looking for escape. The only door was clear across the room. It was too far, and he'd have to get through the grymclaws to reach it.

He turned back to the grymclaws and slowly raised the bone to defend himself. He stopped, surprised to find them staring at the fallen grymclaw on the ground. While their attention was elsewhere, he slowly backed away, hoping they wouldn't notice.

The grymclaw closest to the body screeched and jabbed toward the ground. The one next to her screeched and did the same. Then another. All the grymclaws drew around the fallen one and began tearing her apart with their beaks. A feeding frenzy, Kenric realized with horror.

Slowly, he inched his way across the room to the door. They never looked up. At last his fingers connected with the handle. He turned it slowly, then flung himself through the door.

Once safely outside, Kenric took a moment to catch his breath. His shoulders seemed to have stopped bleeding, but he was covered in dried blood. He'd left his pack in the tower, but there was no way he was going back in there to get it. The dagger was still in the grymclaw's body. He was defenseless and without supplies, stuck in Mordig's fortress.

KENRIC SHOVED ASIDE his exhaustion and pushed away from the wall. His first order of business was to find where they were keeping his father.

The fortress was a maze of towers, courtyards, stairways, and bridges. He'd also discovered that the fortress was crawling with grim-faced guards. After many dead ends, Kenric chose a narrow bridge that led from the turret to an inner courtyard. As he stepped into the courtyard, he heard the clatter of a small party of guards marching toward him. He pressed himself back into the shadowed arch and held his breath. Fear roiled in his gut like a trapped eel. Had they seen him?

"Ho there, Golnir! You're to report to the forge immediately," the guard said.

Kenric's knees almost buckled in relief. They weren't talking to him.

"There's to be a blade testing in the morning, and there's word of an intruder in the village. His Lordship wants to double the guard on the smith from Penrith until the testing."

The smith from Penrith! Kenric's father was here. Relief surged through Kenric, chasing away his exhaustion and dulling his pain. He had found his father.

"Bah!" a voice called back. "That smith from Penrith is a surly fellow. Why don't you guard him yourselves?"

There was a sudden clink of chain mail and the sound of a sword being drawn. "Because the captain asked for you, that's why. Besides, after tomorrow, you'll never have to deal with him again."

"You don't think his blade is going to work, then?"

Kenric heard the clink of chain mail as the messenger shrugged. "None of the others have."

"Well then, you're right. I'd best enjoy my sport with this smith while I've got a chance. By this time tomorrow, he'll most likely be dead."

❊ 12 ❊

Kenric's heart was galloping in his chest. He'd nearly come too late! He had to get his father free tonight.

Hands clammy with fear, Kenric waited for the guards to leave, then crept out of his hiding place. When he saw no one, he went toward the doorway the guards had taken.

He peered down the corridor. It was a stone passage that led to the center of the fortress.

There was no choice but to follow.

It was dim inside. The feeble torchlight on the walls was barely able to pierce the choking darkness.

His whole body strung as tight as a fiddle. Kenric followed the corridor as it twisted downward. After a while, he came upon other passageways that led off the main one. A faint sound reached his ears, the familiar clang of metal striking metal. A smith's hammer!

Kenric stepped into the passage that led toward the sound. The clanging grew louder. Soon red and orange shadows flickered up ahead.

Flattening himself against the wall, he peered around the doorway.

Before him sat the biggest forge he had ever seen. Enormous logs smoldered red and orange. Just in front of the flames stood a large man with sweat pouring down his face. Sparks flew everywhere as he worked.

Kenric's bones almost melted in relief. It was his father.

His father's face held shadows and creases that hadn't been there before. His shoulders slumped with weariness even as he hammered. But Brogan—his father—was alive.

The four new soldiers whom Kenric had followed took up positions near the others. Now eight soldiers guarded his father, two at each wall.

"Hey, smith!" one of the new guards called out. He was a short, squat fellow. "You'd best be sure this one works. You're only getting a second chance because His Lordship couldn't find another smith."

Brogan tightened his grip on the hammer and squared his shoulders. He ignored the taunting guard.

The fellow turned back to the others. "I don't think he's sweating enough, do you? I think he needs to sweat more if he wants that blade to work."

There was a round of rough laughter, then the guard grabbed a torch off the wall. He carried it over to Brogan, who continued to ignore him and focus on his work.

When the guard shoved the torch close to his father's face, Kenric started forward, catching himself just in time. Slowly, Brogan turned his head. There was such loathing in his eyes that Kenric feared he would strike the guard down where he stood.

"Whether the blade succeeds or fails," Brogan said, "at least I won't have to look at your ugly face again."

The guard growled and flung the torch aside. He lunged for Brogan, but was grabbed by another guard, who held him back. "Enough! The smith must finish this blade. Unless you want to explain to His Lordship why not."

Still muttering, the first guard picked up the torch and shoved it at Brogan, as if to burn him.

"Enough, I said!" thundered the captain. "The sooner he finishes the sooner we can all get out of this wretched hole."

Kenric clenched his fists and fumed. He wanted to pound on the walls in frustration. His father was doomed.

If the blade failed, he would die. If it worked, then evil would rule the land forever.

A LONG TIME later, when Kenric's legs had fallen asleep and his wounded shoulders had grown painfully stiff, Brogan finally spoke. "I'm done," he croaked.

"Come on, then," said the captain of the guards. "Back to your quarters till morning." The guards stepped forward and roughly shoved Brogan toward a tunnel.

Clinging to the shadows, Kenric crept across the forge. He paused at the mouth of the tunnel and waited for the guards to get well ahead of him. He couldn't risk being heard.

When he was sure they were far enough ahead, Kenric took a cautious step forward. Without the guards' torches, the tunnel was like a gaping black mouth.

Kenric shook off his thoughts and felt his way along the walls, taking small shuffling steps. One step, then another.

Suddenly his foot stepped out into nothing and he was tumbling through the darkness.

With a bruising thud, he landed. He lay gasping on the floor and forced himself to open his eyes.

The tunnel glowed faintly.

Of course! The moonstone! He crawled over to where it had fallen out of his pocket when he fell. Silently giving thanks to the old man, he reached over and picked it up. When he held the small stone out in front of him like a candle, he saw that he had tumbled down a short flight of steps. Turning away from them, he continued on after the guards.

The tunnel twisted left, then went down two flights of stairs. It twisted right, crossed a stone bridge, then descended five more flights of stairs. Ahead, he heard the groan of metal as a key turned in a lock, then the squeak of rusty hinges. "We'll be back in the morning to take you to the Great Hall."

"Sleep well, smith," one of the guards called out with a nasty laugh.

The door slammed and the key turned again. Loud footsteps moved toward Kenric. He glanced around, frantically looking for a hiding spot. There was an archway twenty paces back. Kenric scrambled back to it, then flattened himself against the wall. Shoving the moonstone deep into his pocket, he waited for the guards to pass. Surely they would hear his heart pounding in his chest.

As they drew closer to Kenric's hiding place, the first

guard stopped, only a few arm's lengths away. "Did you hear that?"

"What?"

The guards stopped walking and strained to listen in the dark.

Kenric's fear turned his legs to lead. He couldn't have moved, even if they found him.

"I don't hear a thing," the captain finally said. "It's probably just the Mawr hounds, scrounging for scraps."

Kenric froze. Mawr hounds? Here? His eyes strained against the darkness, looking for the reddish glow of the hounds' eyes. He shuddered at the memory of their gaping jaws. He could only hope they were kept locked up.

There was a scrape of boots as the guards walked on.

It took a while for Kenric to work up the courage to move from his hiding place. Avoiding the guards was bad enough, but knowing the Mawr hounds were here almost kept him frozen in place.

But then he couldn't help his father.

He finally crept out of hiding and approached the locked door. He went up on tiptoe and tried looking through the small window in the door. He could see nothing.

He fumbled in his pocket, then pulled out the moonstone. In the soft glow, he saw a small, dank cell. His father sat on a stone ledge with his head in his hands. He looked broken and defeated.

"Father," Kenric whispered. "Father? Can you hear me?"

Brogan lifted his head and looked around the cell. Then he groaned and dropped his head back into his hands.

"Father. Over here. The door," Kenric whispered again, this time more urgently.

His father jerked his head up. "Kenric?"

"Yes. It's me."

Brogan got up and staggered over to the door. "Kenric?" His hands gripped the bars on the window, and he peered out. Kenric reached up and placed his hands on his father's.

"What are you doing here?" his father asked.

Kenric's heart swelled with joy and relief. "I've come to fetch you home."

"You traveled all this way? Alone?" His father peered between the bars to see if anyone was with Kenric. His face fell when he saw that Kenric was alone. "You must leave here at once," his father said, his voice stern and harsh.

Kenric felt as if a bucket of ice-cold water had just

been dumped on him. "Not without you! We've got to get you out of there, then we'll go home."

His father gave a short bark of despair. "Impossible. There is no escape from this place. Besides, if Mordig finds you here, he will use you against me. I couldn't bear that. You must leave before they find you."

Kenric thrust his chin forward. "I'm not leaving without you. I didn't travel all this way just to say good-bye."

"Listen to me." Brogan's voice was urgent. "I've been imprisoned here for two months now. I've seen what Mordig does to those who cross him. I can't let anything like that happen to you. Knowing you and your mother were safe has been my one bit of hope in this nightmare. Don't take that from me!"

Kenric's heart nearly split in two. "As long as Mordig rules the land, no one is safe. Can't you see that?" He added gently, "No one."

Brogan was silent for so long that Kenric grew worried. "Father?"

"Of course you are right," Brogan said, his voice bleak.

The defeat in his father's voice squeezed Kenric's heart. "Don't give up! I'll think of something by morning. I promise."

Brogan gripped Kenric's fingers. "I know you want to

help me. But the only way you can help is to leave. I do not want Mordig to find you." He gave Kenric one last squeeze. "I am proud of you, son. Prouder than you will ever know. Give your mother my love."

Kenric raised up on his tiptoes, not wanting to break contact yet. "Promise me that if a chance comes to escape, you'll take it. Promise."

"If I promise, then will you leave here at once and get yourself to safety?" Brogan asked.

"Yes," Kenric said. "If you promise, I'll leave here at once." Kenric was fairly certain that, to his father, safety meant getting out of the fortress altogether and heading for home. But to Kenric, safety just meant finding someplace to hide where the guards wouldn't find him.

Brogan stared at Kenric in silence for a long time. Finally, he answered. "Very well. If a chance comes, I'll take it. But it won't come, so don't get your hopes up."

Kenric didn't argue. His father had promised and that was enough. Now it was up to Kenric to make sure that the chance came.

❧ 13 ❧

His father's despair ate at Kenric as he worked his way back through the tunnels. He hadn't expected him to be so hopeless. He'd thought his father would be overjoyed to see him. Relieved that help had finally come. But no, he just wanted Kenric safe, whatever the cost.

When Kenric finally reached the forge, he stopped to get his bearings. He had no idea what time of night it was. He had to find the Great Hall. That's where the guards had said the testing would take place.

After many false starts and dead ends, Kenric finally found a room that he was sure must be the Great Hall. It was larger than any of the other rooms he had seen. Pillars of stone went all the way around the room and supported an overhanging balcony. A large carved throne sat on a raised platform in the front of the room. Arched doorways stood on both sides of the platform, with a small door just behind the throne.

Kenric climbed the stairs to the balcony that overlooked the hall. He found a hiding place behind a stone pillar that gave him a good view of the front of the room. He settled in to wait.

He couldn't get comfortable. His shoulders ached as if they were on fire, and his stomach was painfully empty. His mind kept going back to his father and how beaten he'd looked. As if some vital force or piece of himself had been stolen from him.

An ugly thought slithered through Kenric's mind. Perhaps this was the first step to becoming a Sleäg. Having your own spirit quenched would make room for the bitter fires Mordig liked to build.

Kenric reached into his pocket and fiddled with the nail that hid there. His father's words came back to him. *Hammering the iron strengthens the blade, much like the hammering of life strengthens the man. Although sometimes, if you hammer too hard too soon, the whole thing will shatter.*

Is that what had happened to his father? Had Mordig shattered him?

No! He wouldn't believe that. Couldn't believe that. Giving in to despair was what Mordig wanted. Kenric might as well get up and hand over his own soul if he was going to think that way.

Kenric leaned his head back and tried to sleep, but he was wound too tightly. Restless, he pulled the small pouch from around his neck. He dumped the two stones out into his hand. Bright red drops flared to life as the bloodstone touched his skin. Next to it, the fire-stone's red gold shimmered faintly in the blue depths. It would need Hnagi's touch to ignite the flames within. He pulled the moon-stone from his chest pocket and put it with the others. All three stones lay in his hand: one each for Fey, man, and goblin.

Guilt flared at the thought of the little goblin. Kenric hadn't had time to look for him. He'd been too busy trying to save his father. But as soon as his father was safe, Kenric vowed he would search for Hnagi.

"What is that you have in your hand?"

Kenric closed his fist and jerked his head up, surprised to see the old man perched on the step next to him. "You!" Kenric whispered. "What are you doing here? And what happened to you? I can see right through you!"

"Have you not guessed yet?" The old man sighed and leaned forward. "What do you think happened to the king when he didn't die, eh? If he didn't die but had no mortal body left, what do you think he might look like?"

Kenric opened his mouth, but no words came out.

The old king—for Kenric now realized that was who he was—nodded. "Exactly. I have been trapped in this ghostly body, unable to do anything to help my kingdom. I have traveled the land looking for answers to old prophecies and ways to forge new power. In my searching, I stumbled upon you."

"Me?"

"I cannot afford to be choosy. Now, show me what you've got in your hand," the old king commanded.

Tightly gripped in his fist, the stones gave off a strange warmth. Slowly, Kenric opened his hand.

A look of awe spread across the king-wraith's face. "You have all three stones! No human has possessed all three stones in over a hundred years!" When he met Kenric's gaze, there was new respect in his eyes. "How do you come to have one of each?"

Thinking he'd done something wrong, Kenric shrugged. "You gave me the moonstone yourself. The fire-stone is from Hnagi, a goblin I was traveling with. The bloodstone was given to me by one of the Fey."

"The Fey gave you that?" the king-wraith asked. He pointed at the bloodstone, looking as if he'd seen a ghost.

Kenric nodded. The king-wraith slowly reached for the stone.

Just then, the doors below crashed open. Kenric jumped at the sound, and the king-wraith jerked his hand back and looked over his shoulder. He turned to Kenric and closed Kenric's hand over the stones. "Keep these!" the king-wraith said urgently. "You will need them."

Kenric dumped the stones into his pocket as a figure strode into the Great Hall below. He was followed by a swarm of guards. Mordig.

He was tall and broad, broader than any man Kenric had ever seen. There was a thickness to him, a bend to his legs and arms that spoke of something not fully human.

His entire body was covered in black armor. At his shoulders, wrists, and elbows sat wicked-looking wings of spiked armor. Kenric couldn't see the warlord's face. It was fully hidden by a helm of black. On top of the helm sat a crown of sharp, curved blades, like the horns of some wild beast. There was a slit for his mouth, and two gaping holes where his eyes should have been. Kenric's stomach began roiling again. He drew farther back into the shadows.

Mordig walked up the three steps that led to his throne and flung himself into the stone chair. His voice ripped through the air. "Let the testing begin!"

A door opened and two rows of guards streamed in. Between the last two shuffled Kenric's father, his feet hobbled with chains. Kenric wanted to slam his fist into someone, something. Stealth and cunning, he reminded himself. These were his tools. Not open confrontation.

His father bore a large, black cushion, which held a magnificent sword. Its long, straight blade winked silver. Would that sword truly give Mordig more power? Kenric wondered. Magnify his will? Kenric shuddered at the thought.

More guards filed in behind Brogan. They all stopped in front of the throne.

Mordig spoke. "Brogan from Penrith, you have been given one last chance to please me. If the blade tests well, you will have all the fame and glory you could wish for. If not, you shall die by the blade you forged. Do you understand?"

Kenric's father nodded his head.

Mordig turned to the guards. "Were the fires hot enough? Did his sweat go into the making of this blade?"

"Aye, my Lord."

Mordig nodded. "Excellent." He steepled his hands. "When we tested the last blade the smith forged, we used human blood. The blade failed. Today, let us try something different. Perhaps a blade of power requires goblin blood."

At his words, two guards dragged a cowering, squealing goblin into the hall.

Hnagi! Kenric almost shouted the name out loud.

Hnagi squealed again as he was dragged closer to the sword. Kenric looked around, trying to think. He had to *do* something. He couldn't let the goblin come to harm. Hnagi was his responsibility.

Just then, Hnagi twisted in the guards' grip. He tried to leap into the large hearth in the far wall, but the guard was too fast. He held the goblin even tighter as one of the other guards lifted the sword from the cushion.

As the sharp point of the sword drew closer to Hnagi, Kenric had an idea.

He ripped Hnagi's pouch off his belt and jerked it open. He heard Hnagi cry out as the tip of the blade drew toward him. Kenric grabbed a handful of the goblin fire-dust and hurled it at the guards.

A loud explosion rocked the Great Hall. With a crackle and roar, flames leaped up from the stone floor. Hnagi and the two guards were immediately swallowed up by flames while the guard holding the sword leaped back to safety.

But flames couldn't hurt the goblin. He cowered in the safety of the fire while the two guards screamed in pain and threw themselves away from the flames.

Ignoring his burning guards, Mordig whipped his head around to stare up at the gallery. Full of fury and hatred, his eyes went straight to Kenric. "Seize him!" he shouted.

Four guards fanned out from behind the throne, heading for the balcony. Kenric turned to run, then froze as he saw Mordig stride into the flames.

His plan had failed!

Seconds later, Mordig reappeared, dragging the little goblin behind him. He shoved Hnagi toward the guard with the blade. "Do it!" he commanded.

The guard reached forward and slashed the goblin's palm. Hnagi screamed and tried to pull his arm back, but Mordig held fast. He squeezed the goblin's hand until blood ran down the length of the blade.

Kenric stood frozen to the spot, waiting to see if the goblin's blood would give the blade the power Mordig was looking for.

Nothing happened.

In disgust, Mordig flung Hnagi across the room. He looked up and pointed at Kenric. "Bring him to me," he called out.

❖ 14 ❖

KENRIC TURNED TO run, but two guards appeared at the far end of the balcony. He turned the other way, and found two more guards blocking that escape as well.

The two closest guards grabbed Kenric and wrenched his arms back. They shoved him toward the stairs. He stumbled, trying to keep his balance.

They dragged him down the stairs and over to Mordig, who towered over him. Kenric stared up into the evil-looking helmet and felt Mordig's anger rush over him in a red-hot wave.

"No! Please!" Brogan called out. A hush fell over the room.

Mordig turned to the blacksmith. "This boy means something to you?"

Brogan looked at Kenric. "He is my son, and I plead for your mercy."

There was a dead silence, then Mordig threw back his head and laughed. Thick ropes of fear knotted in Kenric's stomach at the harsh, chilling sound. There was no mercy here.

"How perfect! I can use the blood of an apprentice smith to test the blade and still have a master smith left over to try again if it should fail!"

Kenric's father looked as if he'd been struck.

Mordig motioned to the guards. "Let's test the blade and be done with it!" He turned, strode back to his throne and sat down.

The four guards dragged Kenric toward the guard holding the sword. He fought them, but it was no use.

The guards wrestled him until he was standing directly in front of the blade. He wanted to look to his father for courage. But he was afraid to meet his eyes now that he'd failed.

Three of the guards held him down while the fourth grabbed his arm, pulling it closer to the blade. Again, he struggled, but the guard was too strong. He forced Kenric's hand forward until it touched the tip of the sword.

A quick burning slashed across his palm. Red blood oozed up. The guard reached out and squeezed Kenric's hand until one fat drop welled up, then slowly rolled onto the tip of the blade.

Kenric heard a faint sizzle, then the smell of hot metal filled his nostrils.

"It's working," whispered the guard, loosening his grip on Kenric's shoulders.

The tip of the blade suddenly blazed with a blinding white fire. As Kenric reeled in pain and confusion, a voice spoke in his head. *Sweat is to make it, blood is to bind it, strike first in love, so evil can't find it.* He looked up to the balcony. The king-wraith leaned against the railing. He jerked his head in Brogan's direction, then looked back at Mordig.

Puzzled, Kenric frowned.

"Strike first in love," the voice boomed inside his skull. *"So evil can't find it."*

Horror flooded through Kenric. The king-wraith meant for him to strike his father with the sword! *Strike first in love.* Kenric looked up at the king-wraith and shook his head frantically.

"Strike first in love, so evil can't find it!" the king-wraith

shouted inside Kenric's head. "You have no choice, lad. Will your father be safe if the kingdom is still in the hands of evil?"

Kenric cringed, certain all had heard the words. But everyone was still watching the sizzling white fire work its way up the blade.

Kenric turned to look at his father as the full weight of his choice sank in. His hand found its way to his pocket and his fingers closed around the nail he'd carried with him from Penrith. So it all came down to this. He could save his father or save the kingdom from Mordig's evil. He had risked so much, come so far, only to have to make such a terrible choice.

"Sweat is to make it, blood is to bind it, strike first in love, so evil can't find it." This time the king-wraith's voice rang throughout the hall for everyone to hear.

Heads jerked up, trying to locate the voice. While everyone was distracted, Kenric gripped the nail firmly. He pulled it out of his pocket, then stabbed the guard's hand.

The guard bellowed in pain and let go of the sword.

Kenric lunged forward and caught the blade before it hit the ground.

The magic of it crackled through his hands, making them tingle.

Kenric turned the sword on the injured guard. The crackling white fire flared along the blade. Clutching his hand, the soldier stepped back. The other guards drew back also, as if they were afraid of the power the blade held.

Mordig looked from Kenric to the blade to Brogan. "Kill the smith! Quickly! Before the power of the sword is lost!" he ordered his guards.

Kenric raised the sword high over his shoulder. His arms shook with the weight of his choice. *Strike first, strike first, strike first* echoed in his head.

Out of the corner of his eye, Kenric saw guards rushing toward his father, swords drawn. His father was a dead man.

Strike first, strike first, strike first.

Suddenly, from deep inside, he heard a voice. Not the king-wraith's voice, but that of his father. *Your knowledge of the metal and its secrets, your willingness to give the blade what it wants, will make it great.*

He would give the blade what it wanted. But he would force it down a path of his own choosing, as well.

He swung. The blade flashed silver as it arced through the air. As the blade drew closer to his father, Kenric twisted the hilt, just a half turn. The razor-sharp edge of the blade turned from his father's neck. The flat of the blade struck Brogan full across the shoulders, knocking him to the floor.

"Noooo!" Mordig cried, jerking to his feet.

There was a sizzling, burning feeling in Kenric's hands. He looked down to see the blinding white light had turned into a small, crackling blue flame racing down the blade.

A small flame could bring down a cottage.

Or a warlord.

Almost as if the blade itself were pulling him, Kenric turned and charged at Mordig. The force of Kenric's rage carried him up the three steps to Mordig's throne. The tip of the blue-flamed sword pierced Mordig's armor and went all the way through his shoulder. Off balance, Mordig stumbled back onto the throne.

A loud crack rang out through the hall as the sword struck stone, then sank into it as easily as if it were butter.

Mordig bellowed in rage. He flailed at Kenric, but his armor limited his movements. Kenric held fast to the sword and dodged the blows as best he could.

"The stones, boy!" the king-wraith called out. "Do you have them?"

Kenric nodded. He watched with mounting panic as Mordig put his hands on the blade, trying to pull it out. The blue flame crackled and flared at the warlord's touch. With a roar of pain, he jerked his hands away.

Kenric held the hilt with one hand and reached into his pocket with the other.

Mordig swung his free arm at Kenric's head.

Kenric ducked. The warlord's arm sailed over his head as his hand closed firmly over the three stones in his pocket.

"Quickly, repeat after me."

Kenric glanced to the side and saw the king-wraith standing next to him.

"Hurry now! The power is fading!"

Kenric looked down at the blade. The blazing blue-white light was growing fainter.

The king-wraith's voice murmured in his ear. "By the power of the earth, moon, and fire, I bind you to this stone as I bind you to my king's will, that you may do nothing against Lowthar as long as he shall live."

Kenric took a deep breath. "By the power of the earth, moon, and fire, I bind you to this stone as I bind you to my king's will, that you may do nothing against Lowthar as long as he shall live," he repeated.

As he finished speaking, the stone behind Mordig screamed, as if it were being ripped apart.

Mordig shouted in surprise as he began to sink into the throne as if it were quicksand. He struggled, trying to lift his arms, then his feet; but they were stuck fast to the melting stone behind him.

Kenric turned to the king-wraith, who was no longer a wraith. As Mordig's body was swallowed up by the stone, the king's body flowed back into his ghostly self, like sand filling up an hourglass.

There was a flurry of motion behind him in the great chamber. Some of the guards fell to their knees, while others fled. Still others simply faded into nothingness, leaving empty piles of chain mail behind. It was as if their very bodies went with Mordig into the stone.

"Mordig's constructs," the king said close to Kenric's ear. "Creatures of his making that are bound to his will."

"Noooo!" The warlord gave one final wail as he disappeared into the stone. The sword hilt blazed one last time, then turned to dust and fell to the ground.

The king turned and looked at Kenric. "That was Mordig's mistake. When he struck me down with the blade of power, he neglected to bind my physical body to the earth, or my will to his. He left my spirit free to roam the land, looking for answers."

Kenric looked down at the three small stones he held in his hand. "So these stones gave the sword the power to do all that?"

"Yes. They lent the full weight of the kingdom to the king's will," the king explained. "The light of the Fey, the fire of the goblins, and the blood of man, all united in a single purpose. Our land's power lies in the strength of these alliances. The balance of power among the three races has been sorely broken and must be mended."

Kenric felt a hand on his shoulder. He turned to find his father standing behind him. Brogan reached down and swept Kenric into his arms, squeezing tight. "I am so proud of you," he said fiercely.

His father held him so long that Kenric felt the tips of his ears grow pink with embarrassment.

"Sire." A soldier addressed the king. Kenric pulled back from his father and saw that the soldier carried a small, limp form.

"Hnagi!" Kenric cried. He remembered the little goblin being flung across the hall. Kenric left his father and rushed over to the soldier. He grabbed the goblin's hand.

It was cold and still. Dread settled heavily in Kenric's heart. The little goblin didn't deserve this. He'd only been trying to help Kenric.

A small black eye opened. "Big meanie gone for good?"

Relief bubbled through Kenric. He couldn't decide whether to bop the goblin on the head or hug him. "You scared me! I thought you were dead!"

"No. Hnagi just play dead. Wait until safe." The little goblin shuddered. "Ken-ric kill Mordig?"

"Well, yes and no. He's not fully dead." Kenric looked over his shoulder at the mound of stone that sat where the throne used to be. "But I don't think he'll be harming any goblins for a long time."

The king's voice boomed across the chamber as he turned to face the rest of the guards and soldiers. "You have seen the true power return to Tirga Mor this day. Throw down your weapons of evil. Lay aside your bitterness and hurt. Let us rejoin once again and turn back to the old alliances."

Murmurs ran through the soldiers. Here and there, voices cheered.

"Go forth and spread the word. Mordig is gone. His evil is no more." The men began filing out of the chamber, hastening to spread the word.

"Aren't you afraid they'll turn on you? How can you trust them after they've served Mordig?" Kenric asked.

"Most were not bad, just weak," the king explained. "Some even held out hope that something would stem the tide of Mordig's rule. All it took was a spark, one thing they could rally behind. Something to remind them, deep in their hearts, of who and what they truly were." He turned the full force of his gaze to Kenric.

Kenric squirmed in embarrassment and pleasure under the weight of that gaze.

"Ken-ric," Hnagi said with a sly smile. Then he reached out and pinched him.

THE ADVENTURE CONTINUES IN BOOK 2

THE SECRETS OF GRIM WOOD

Kenric's adventure continues in Book 2 of the *Lowthar's Blade* trilogy, *The Secrets of Grim Wood:*

THE LARGE DOORS swung open, and a servant appeared. "The king will see you now."

Kenric and his father stepped into King Thorgil's chambers. The king sat at a desk cluttered with parchments and scrolls. He put down his quill and rubbed his eyes as they entered. "There is much to be dealt with, as you can imagine."

"We understand, Your Majesty," Brogan said.

"We will be one less thing for you to worry about as soon as you give us permission to leave for home," Kenric added.

"Anxious to get home, young smith?"

"Yes, Your Majesty."

The king picked up his quill and began twirling it in

his hand. "You have done much to serve your kingdom, but now I'm afraid I must ask even more of you."

Not liking the sound of this one bit, Kenric shuffled his feet.

"You have bound Mordig and his evil to the stone," the king said. "But binding is tied to my will. It will last only as long as I live, and I do not know how much longer that will be."

The king got up out of his chair and began pacing. "Furthermore, there is too much here that I don't understand. I do not know why Mordig was able to use my sword against me. Or why the blow didn't kill me. I certainly had no idea that I would return to my physical body once Mordig was stripped of his power.

"Even worse, I don't know what has happened to the blade. Has it been destroyed? Or is it ensorcelled and waiting for us to find it?"

The king was silent for a moment, then spoke again. "We must find answers. For centuries, the kings of Lowthar thought we held the true blade of power. It appears we were wrong. If there really is a true blade of power, then we must find it. If not, then we must find a way to forge one. We need a blade that will rid us of Mordig's evil and secure Lowthar forever.

"And there is something else," King Thorgil added, a sad look passing over his face. "We must find the rightful heir to the throne. We must find the princess, Tamaril."

Princess! Kenric didn't know there was a princess!

"Your daughter?" Brogan asked. "But she died five years ago, right after you did. Or when we all thought you did."

Thorgil shook his head. "No. The princess was already making her escape when Mordig stormed the fortress. She used the maze of underground tunnels to flee the castle."

"Well, can't she just come back?" Kenric asked.

"Ah, but that is the problem. I have no idea where she has gone or how to get word to her now that Mordig's reign has ended."

Kenric's heart sank. They would never find her without some clue where to look.

"I am hoping she ran away to Grim Wood," the king continued. "That is the best place to go if one wishes to get lost. Tamaril would have known that. But she may not even be alive any longer, for all I know."

With great effort, the king pulled himself out of his black thoughts. "May I see your bloodstone?"

Surprised, Kenric took it out of his pocket. The drops of red shone brightly as Kenric handed it to the king.

Gently, almost lovingly, King Thorgil held the bloodstone in his hand. "How did you come by this?" he asked so softly that Kenric had to lean forward to hear him.

"A Fey girl gave it to me in Grim Wood, Your Majesty."

The king's head jerked up, and he pierced Kenric with his sharp gaze. "You're sure she was Fey?"

A brief image of Linwe, her hair full of leaves and twigs, her pointed ears and sharp teeth, flashed in his mind. "Yes, Your Majesty. Positive."

Silence stretched out between them before the king spoke again. "This was Tamaril's stone," he said at last. "Hers was oval-shaped like this one, and about this size." Hope flared briefly in his bleak face. "That could mean that she made it as far as Grim Wood."

"But the Fey . . ." Kenric began.

"She had a moonstone to guarantee her safe passage. Maybe they will know where she has gone."

The king handed the bloodstone back to Kenric. Then he put his hands on Kenric's shoulders. "Which is just one of the reasons I am appointing you my ambassador to the Fey. You have already won their respect, so they should trust you more easily than most. It is time to begin mending the old alliances. All the races must unite in order to defeat Mordig's threat to our land.

"The Fey are well known for their love of ancient lore. You must go into the heart of Grim Wood and find out everything they know about the blades of power and how to forge them. See if they will help us in this task. They may even have some knowledge of Mordig and how to defeat him. While you are there, see if anyone has word of the princess and knows what might have become of her."

Kenric squirmed. He longed to be home. He couldn't wait to see the look on his mother's face when she saw Father. Or the look on Gormley's face when he came to kick them out of their cottage, only to find himself face-to-face with the brawny blacksmith.

But as much as he wanted to, he couldn't refuse a direct order of the king. Kenric hated to think what would happen to the kingdom if Mordig broke free. He knew all too well what evil would be unleashed upon the land. And there was no doubt whom Mordig would come after first.

Besides, the king had aided him in rescuing his father.

Kenric owed it to him to try to help put his family back together.

Kenric took a deep breath. "Yes, Your Majesty. I will do as you command."